UNASSUMED

Zara Zee and the Unassuming Case of the Billionaire Heir

An Adult Action Adventure Mystery Thriller

Kailin Gow

UNASSUMED

DEDICATION

To my mom, who introduced me to the world of movies, martial arts, and making the most of myself despite or in spite of being "just a girl". There are many strong women in the world, especially in Asia, and hopefully Zara Zee embodies some of them.

Prologue

Officer Zara Zee
Hong Kong – at Lu Towers

"I am in the basement of Lu Towers, and let me tell you, Peter, the building may cost 1.5 billion dollars to build, but from down here, it looks like I'm the bowels of a mechanical steam dragon. It's a maze down here. Are you sure the signal is coming from this building?" Zara asked her superior Peter Brock through the cellphone. "It's Richard Lu's own building, where he has his office on the penthouse floor. You mean he was held in his own building the entire time he was kidnapped?"

"It's where the signal is coming from," Peter said, his British accent clipped and his tone short. "Be careful, Zara. Richard Lu is a well-trained martial artist. He was tutored by the best money could afford since he was a child. If these people could capture him and hold him hostage, they must be professionals. These people don't kid around. They mean business."

"I got that," Zara said. Zara held both hands around the handle of her colt .45 ready to shoot at anyone coming down the half-lit hallway in the basement for one of Hong Kong's most beautifully designed state-of-the-art high-rises known as Lu's Towers.

Why wasn't the basement as lit as the rest of the flashy building? Lu Towers was known for its changing neon light patterns that lit up the entire building for miles. A winner of many architectural design competition, Lu Towers was touted as a major and exciting new addition to the cosmopolitan Hong Kong cityscape.

You would think the basement would be high-tech and glamorous too.

Not this grim dungeon-like maze where the lights weren't working, and it reeked of gasoline, sulfur, garbage, and rotting food. It was a ghastly combination of a smell, and Zara tried to block out the intense odor.

She held out her gun but walked carefully in the near dark until she saw a glimpse of green neon light coming from around the corner.

Zara had to hold her breath. The smell was ten times more intense here.

She waited for any sound, but it has been quiet for the past few minutes she had made her way to the basement. She followed the green light which illuminated the basement with a faint eeriness that reminded her of those old horror films she had watched growing up with her old-fashion grandmother. It had only been about ten to fifteen years ago when she first moved to live with her grandmother in a humble little one-bedroom house in a small town just outside of Hong Kong. She was only five but she remembered how scared and sad she was when her grandmother took her in, following the accident that killed both her parents. Her grandmother was poor, and the house barely had electricity. What she did have was some change, which she gave Zara, to have her go to an old one screen theater playing classic films from the United States. A neighbor of her grandmother took her to the theater while her grandmother talked to the police who brought Zara to her. Frankenstein was the black and white film she had to watch that day.

Zara gripped her gun tightly. She had a feeling she was going to make a discovery on the other side of the door where the main source of the green light was coming from.

Her cellphone vibrated, and she answered it without saying a word. She had it go to text instead.

Peter was on the line: *Zara, you are right where the signal is strongest. We have a team who will be there in a minute. They would be there sooner but traffic is a killer. Thank God you were right at the café nearby when we got the signal. Wait for them, and they will give you backup.*

Zara was already at the door, the cellphone in her pocket. A humming noise was coming from the room. Then a soft scraping. Maybe a shoe against the floor. Someone was in there.

How many of them were in there? Who was in there? Did they have Richard Lu?

Zara was about to reach for her cellphone to ask Peter if he can get an id on the maintenance workers for Lu Towers. It didn't make sense that Richard Lu would be down here. There was no business for him here, with him being far removed from his operations people. Unless he knew them.

"Ahhh!" Zara heard the man's faint voice grimace in pain. Zara remembered seeing Richard Lu on television once when he rang the bell for the Hong Kong stock market.

He was a handsome and large man, the recent heir to his family's fortunes and successor to the Lu Legacy of real estate, hospitality, foreign investment and more. He also had a distinct deep voice. It was just a groan, but she could tell it belonged to Richard Lu.

She kicked open the door, and quickly looked around the room, expecting a gang of men to fire at her or to jump her.

But the place was empty except for a wooden chair next to the furnace. A cord leading from the furnace to the man sitting in the chair, slumped down. Bloodied, a cellphone on and vibrating in his shirt pocket. It was the source of the green light.

Zara almost threw up.

He couldn't reach his phone because his fingers were cut off. He couldn't hear her coming to shout for help because his ears were cut off. His one good eye stared bloodily at her while the other was shut closed.

Feces and old food littered the area around him.

"Hold on!" Zara shouted, running to him.

But as soon as stepped onto the rubberized mat that covered the area near the door, a signal went off, and the cord next to Richard was ignited from the furnace with a spark of fire that quickly traveled down to Richard.

Richard could see the fire light up and he seemed to be shouting at Zara, "Get out!" Zara saw him indicate his head at the cellphone in his pocket. A bomb? The cellphone?

Zara tried to get to him to snatch it but it took less than a second before Richard was completely engulfed in flames and then the room began shaking.

The bomb wasn't on Richard. It wasn't the cellphone. It was under Richard's chair. There was a matt underneath his chair. Any slight movement would set it off, which was why he didn't try to call out to anyone or try to escape.

Zara began rushing to him, saving him was the only thought in her mind, but strong arms held her back.

Peter. The rest of their team was behind him.

"I can save him!" Zara shouted, trying to rush back in, but Peter pulled her back.

"Everyone, run! This place is going to explode!"

Peter grabbed her hand, and they were running down the hallway with the two officers behind them before the entire room exploded, along with the basement.

Zara and Peter were running as fast as they could, exiting out to the street through an emergency exit door, but they turned around and the two officers behind them were no longer behind them.

"Kenneth! Thomas!" Peter shouted, running in, but Zara held him back.

The entire basement was like a giant furnace with fire everywhere.

A loud alarm sounded, sending everyone into a panic. People were pouring out of the building. The fire truck was already there, and everywhere she looked, there was chaos and disorder. Even if they tried to go back in to look for Kenneth and Thomas, the crowd of people running for their lives pushing their way out of the building, blocked them from entering.

"Peter...they doused him with gasoline and filled the basement with it. He was down there for days, undergoing such torture. They weren't merciful, those bastards. He paid them already. They got his ransom, yet they still did all that to him and killed him."

She was crying now. It wasn't like her to lose it on the job. She was more professional than that. She didn't even know Richard Lu, except for his celebrity persona as a billionaire heir.

But Zara was the last person he saw before he died. She couldn't forget the look in his eyes before he was engulfed.

"Kenneth and Thomas, too." Peter was shaking. "The fire came at us so fast, we barely made it out ourselves."

"Who can be so cruel?" Zara asked.

"All the evidence from the kidnapping blew up in there," Peter said.

Zara looked down. If only she had waited for back up. If only she didn't rush into the room and stepped on the matt, triggering the fire that led to igniting the explosive on Richard. She clenched her hand into a tight fist. It was not only cruel to make Richard suffer like that, but to have him witness his own beloved pride and joy building go up in flames. "Whoever they are," Zara said bitterly. "I will make them pay."

Chapter 1

1 month later

Leopold Lee
Hong Kong – At the Oyster House Restaurant

Leopold Lee walked through the sea of tuxedos and elegant gowns, eager to get celebrity chef Errol King's take on the night so far. Women stopped him to whisper sweet promises into his ear, while the men clamped their hands over his in sincere congratulations. It was a big night, one that all of Hong Kong had been waiting for.

The opening of the Oyster House had been the talk of the town for several weeks with many anticipating a world class meal created by the one and only Errol King. There were also a few hard to please critics who would be quick to slash their hopes for success if the tiniest detail was ignored. Some had even gone so far as to openly wish them a huge failure.

"Wipe that worry off your face," Errol said the minute Leo approached him. "Everything is going great. We're a hit."

"Do you think we'll have enough oysters?"

"Yes. It's the quantity of champagne you should be worried about."

"Really?" Panic almost took hold of his heart at the thought.

"No," Errol said with a laugh. "Relax."

"That's easy for you to say. This isn't your home town."

"Yeah, but my reputation is still on the line."

Leo shook his head with uncertainty. "The night is far from over and so much can go wrong still." Sucking his cheeks in as he scanned the large room, he shoved his hands into the pockets of his tuxedo slacks and looked around him. "We promised them a fusion of French and Chinese cuisine."

"Not only in the preparation of the food, but look at this décor. It reflects perfectly this meeting of East and West, old and new, modern and traditional."

Leo looked up at the pearl laden chandeliers hung high in the central portion of the ceiling that rose to almost twenty feet. The thousands of pearls glimmered beneath strategically placed lighting worthy of the hottest nightclub.

"Mr. Lee," a short man said as he came up behind them. "Mr. King. You're just the men I'd like to talk to."

Leo forced a pleased and relaxed smile. "What can we do for you?"

"I'm Frankie Cheung, and I write *Eat Out Hong Kong*."

"The blog?" Errol said with an impressed cock of his brow.

Frankie nodded. "I have quite a following, and I'm sure my readers will be eager to see what I think of your bold endeavor. First off, I'd like to congratulate you on your opening night."

Leo and Errol nodded.

"Before I go off on how fabulous I find the food, I was just wondering what brought an American action movie hero slash heir to one of the most profitable conglomerates in all of China together with a world renowned French chef?"

Errol laughed and clamp his hand over Frankie's shoulder. "Leo and I go way back, but I don't think it's the story you really want." He swept two champagne flutes off the silver platter brought around by one of the dozens of waiters and waitresses working the floor that night. Handing them to Leo and Frankie, he picked another one up for himself and raised it. "A toast; to good food, good company and many great reviews."

"I'll drink to that." Frankie gulped down the contents and looked around. "A lot of people question whether Hong Kong needs another luxury restaurant with that East meets West flavor. Do you think you'll be able to compete with places such as Caprice, Chez Patrick and La Cabane?"

"We know we've got some tough competition," Errol said, "but we're confident there's room in Hong Kong for another fine cuisine restaurant."

"And we do have a few distinguishing factors," Leo added. "Our décor is both luxurious and hip, but also traditional. He glanced down at the red marble flooring beneath his feet.

"Good fortune," Frankie said in recognition of the color's significance.

Leo nodded. "And as you can see... or rather hear, we've hired Bai Tseun, an exquisite violinist who'll be the first in a long line of artists to accompany diners' meals."

Errol nudged Leo with his elbow. "I'll go check how things are going in the kitchen."

Leo nodded as he picked up another champagne flute from a passing waiter, setting his empty flute on the platter. "And if you'll excuse me," he said to Frankie. "I'll make the rounds to ensure everyone is having a good time."

"Good talking to you."

Happy with his impromptu interview with the blogger, Leo meandered through the crowd who showered him with words of praise and promises to return to The Oyster House again and again. Proud of what he'd accomplished with Errol and Eddie, the Chinese chef personally trained by Errol himself, he sipped his champagne and tried to enjoy the moment.

The flight from Paris had been long, and since getting off the plane he'd been in a whirlwind of preparations that often seemed as complicated as they were tiresome. Leaning against the glass door that opened onto the Chinese rock garden, he emptied his champagne flute and reached for another when a waitress came by. He had been away from Hong Kong for a while, filming and living his life away from his family fortune and expectations. Now he was back, and Oyster House was one big reason why…a venture he could call his own. He wanted to make a name for himself besides being his father's son, the heir to his father's legacy. Now that Oyster House was off to a fine start, he could relax. The night couldn't run more perfectly, he thought as he took a sip.

So far the press seemed happy enough with the restaurant, the critics were impressed, and the A-list guests were visibly enjoying themselves. In addition to the flutes of champagne and wine that circulated the large restaurant were platters of oysters, various hors d'oeuvre and mini portions of the many items from the menu.

Fifteen minutes later, when Errol had yet to emerge from the kitchen, Leo headed down to see if any problems had kept him tied up. As he made his way, he once again grabbed a flute of champagne.

"How's everything going in here?" he said as he entered the bustling kitchen.

Errol took one look at him and grinned. "Running like a well-oiled machine. You'd think everyone had been working with us for years. How are you holding up?"

"Great. I'm having a great time."

"I think you might be having too much of a good time."

"Hey, man. The past twenty-four hours, no, forty-eight hours have been among the most stressful in a long time and I deserve a few gulps of champagne."

Errol laughed. "Don't underestimate that stuff. Properly chilled it's delectably refreshing, but when it hits... watch out."

Around them, employees scrambled to supply the growing crowd with a constant flow of fine food. It was a moment of fulfillment and true contentment for Leo. After so much hardship, the loss of his father, inheriting the overwhelmingly successful company his father had founded, and now opening a restaurant with a celebrity chef, it felt good to finally let go and enjoy himself.

When a waitress came in to fill her tray with a fresh batch of champagne flutes, Leo glanced at Errol who shrugged and chuckled.

"It's your head, man," Errol said. "And I can tell you, tomorrow you're going to wish it wasn't."

Leo grabbed a flute, but he didn't have time to drink it down that Errol's word proved too true. The flute slipped through his fingers and crashed to the floor and the buzz of employees around him was suddenly too much.

"And there you go." Putting his arm around Leo, he patted his shoulder as he guided him out of the kitchen and to the right of the noise filled dining room. "Go sleep it off. I'll keep an eye on the place."

"But there's still so much to do," Leo argued as he struggled to climb the steps to the second floor.

"Nothing I can't handle. Besides, you wouldn't want the press to get a shot of you walking around tipsy. Sleep it off, and I'll come around later to give you an update."

Errol pushed the door to the large private lounge above the restaurant and settled Leo on the cushy leather sofa that took almost the entire far wall to the right. "Take it easy."

"Hey," Leo called out before Errol walked out. "Thanks... for everything."

UNASSUMED

Laughing, Errol waved off the words of gratitude. "After what you did in Paris to help me out, it's the least I could do. Besides I want Oyster House to do well. We're partners, and when it does well, everyone's happy. Now get some sleep. You're supposed to be at Lee Holdings first thing tomorrow morning."

Through hooded eyes, Leo looked around him and let out a satisfied sigh. The night had gone off without a hitch and he was relaxing in the lounge he'd had built for this precise reason; to relax. With the walls painted a dark charcoal and the lighting dim and relaxing, it was the perfect place to sit down and think when the whirlwind of the kitchen became too much... at least that'd been the plan when he'd designed it.

Now, as he fought to stay awake, he was happy he'd decided to go with such a soothing décor. Even the couch, with its soft leather and cushiony comfort already proved to be a good investment. It took barely a minute for him to lose his fight to stay awake.

Chapter 2

The large, brightly lit corner office at Lee Holdings, the billion dollar conglomerate his father built up was too much for Leo's aching head and he had to close the blinds on the beautiful view of Victoria Harbor. Gazing out the other wall of windows that offered a view of some of the most beautiful buildings in Hong Kong, he decided to leave the blinds partially open until the morning sun rounded the corner. On any other day he would have appreciated the morning sun that accompanied his first cup of coffee, but the headache Errol had promised him maintained a stronghold.

Sitting behind the large red ivory topped desk, he fingered the soft black leather of the chair that had belonged to his father, a reminder of the responsibility he'd inherited. He sipped his gold rimmed cup of rich gourmet coffee and sighed as he thought of the day ahead. He had time to ponder; despite the hangover that plagued him he'd arrived at his office bright and early, as he had every morning since taking over Lee Holdings Group, a couple of weeks ago.

His father's shoes were big ones, and the pile of folders on his desk reminded him that he had another long day ahead of him. He would have liked nothing more than a day of easy meetings with plenty of time for a nap in between, but that wasn't to be.

After a brief, sharp knock at the door, a pretty brunette with long wavy hair, bright eyes, and a sweet smile walked in wearing a clingy red dress that made him stopped whatever he was doing midway. "Good morning, Mr. Lee."

She had a cute little body with delectable curves, but Leo had no idea who she was. "Where's Mrs. Huang?"

The cute brunette came up to his desk and dumped a stack of files atop the already high pile. "Mrs. Huang had to go to Shanwei. Her niece is having her first baby and she wanted to be there to help her."

"Why wasn't I informed of this?"

"The baby wasn't due for another month yet and Mrs. Huang didn't have time to discuss it with you."

"So you're going to be my new assistant until she gets back?"

"Do you have an objection?"

"No. No, of course not."

"Good." She turned to leave and Leo couldn't take his eyes off her tone backside. Swathed in the clingy fabric of her dress, the perfectly round mounds demanded to be spanked, and he longed to submit himself to that demand. She left the office and returned moments later with another armful of files.

"Miss?"

"Yes," she said as she dumped the files on his desk.

"What do I call you?"

"Zara . Zara Zee."

"Zara . What's all this?"

"The first three are lawsuits. Apparently someone found a piece of metal wiring in a bottle of hand lotion. Cut themselves pretty bad. A few others jumped in on that one claiming to have found wiring in their bottles of lotion as well. Then you have a pile of security clients who aren't satisfied with the way things have been handled since the death of your father. And finally, these..." She ran her fingers along the rest of the pile. "These are suppliers who want payment… now."

Rubbing his eyes with both hands, he groaned then looked up at her. "Why didn't you bring those to the accounting department?"

"Copies have been sent, but I thought it important you know about each of them. They're hefty sums."

"Great."

"I also got a call yesterday from someone who'd like to meet with you to discuss a few investment opportunities."

Annoyed with the amount of work she brought him, he said, "Are you aware that I had a big opening last night?"

"The Oyster House. Yeah, I heard about that. Did everything go well?"

He nodded. "Did you hear that it ran pretty late?"

"Would you rather I come back with these later?"

He flicked open the first file. "No."

"Maybe I could bring you more coffee."

"That'd be nice."

She brought his cup to the elegant recess that housed not only the coffee machine, but also a mini wine cellar with some of the best wine money could buy. Placing a coffee tab in the machine, she pressed the button and waited as the rich brew filled the cup.

It gave Leo another chance to admire her beautiful curves, reminding him how long it'd been since he'd been with a woman. With all the turmoil in his life these past months, hooking up with a girl hadn't really been on his list of priorities, and his body was now taking revenge for that negligence.

His groin stiffened uncomfortably, and he was thankful for the desk that kept that information from her.

"I forgot to mention," she said as she turned to bring him his coffee.

Leo caught her gaze for a second and knew he'd been caught eyeing her. The hint of a pleased smile touched her lips, but she remained otherwise professional.

"You have a meeting with the head of LLG, Mrs. Fong, just before lunch."

"Damn. Who scheduled that?" He wasn't in the habit of giving his assistant a hard time, but he found himself longing to dominate her.

She kept her eyes to the floor, like the good little subservient she was. Maybe losing Mrs. Huang wouldn't be so bad after all.

"If you'll permit me to say, Mr. Lee, this is a very important meeting and…" She cleared her throat. "Perhaps you should consider…"

"Please, Miss Zee. Could you just spit it out?"

"My apologies. "Your suit, sir. It's looking a little… frumpy."

Surprised by her comment, he looked down at his attire and tiredly closed his eyes just as quickly. "Damn it." In his haste, or brain fog, he'd kept his tuxedo slacks he'd slept in and had topped it with a dark blue blazer that had seen better days. To top it off, his beautiful Hermes tie had a neat stain just under the knot.

"I'm sorry, sir."

His eyes angry, he stood and looked down at her. "Start the shower for me."

Nodding, she retreated to the large private bathroom. In the best of times, a meeting with Mrs.

28

Fong wasn't pleasant. If he'd arrived at the meeting looking as he did, it would not have boded well with the strict matriarch.

Squinting, he staggered into the bathroom to find Zara setting up the toiletries he'd need.

"No offense, Mr. Lee, but you don't look very good."

"I might have had one glass of champagne too many."

"Here," she said when he fumbled with his tie. "Let me help you with that."

The erection he'd managed to subdue returned the moment she put her hand to his tie. The motion of her fingers captivated him, and when she pulled the tie over his head and proceeded to unbutton his shirt, every brush of her fingers against his skin burned him.

"I bet you didn't think helping me out of my clothes would be part of the job."

Zara pressed a tight grin and pulled his shirt over his shoulders. "My job is to assist you in whatever capacity I can."

"Good to know. I have a few capacities I'd like to discuss with you later," he said with a deep, hungry tone.

UNASSUMED

His torso bare, he fixed his gaze on hers as she discreetly scanned his chest. With the quick trip to Paris and the opening night of The Oyster House, he hadn't had time to work out as he usually did and he wondered if his muscles showed signs of neglect.

The quick, shy lick of her lips told him she was pleased with what she saw, and her admiration for him further ignited the fire burning through his pants.

My God, he thought. *What is she going to think if she helps me out of my pants and comes face to face with my hard-on?*

He held his breath as she unbuckled his belt, unfastened his pants and pulled them down to his ankles. She didn't bat an eye when faced with the dense bulge in his tight red boxer briefs. Heady from the effect of her proximity, the sweet, heavenly scent of her perfume and the remains of his hangover, he staggered back and reached out to the counter for support.

"Hold onto me," Zara offered as she slipped his arm around her neck and led him to the steamy shower.

Just when he thought she might slip in and join him, she pulled his arm off her and turned him to the shower. "I think you can handle it from here."

He straightened up and forced himself to remain steady, though he wanted to argue his need for her.

"I'll be back to help you into a fresh suit in fifteen minutes."

"Five minutes should be more than enough."

"You're looking a little green around the gills. I suggest you take your time. Mrs. Fong won't be amused if you arrive at this meeting with your faculties less than optimum." She left him in the shower stall and headed back to his office.

Of all the days to be hung over. As the water flowed over his shoulders and down his back, he tapped his forehead to the shower wall and promised himself never to make that mistake again. Regardless of what was happening in his life, he had to keep his head. The next time champagne, or any alcohol was served, he'd limit himself to his usual one or two drinks.

Zara had been right he realized as he slowly washed his hair then lathered up to completely wash away the ill effects of the night before. But as the warm water revitalized him, he found himself thinking more and more of Zara and her wickedly sexy body.

UNASSUMED

Mrs. Huang was an efficient and hard working woman in her early fifties. While he'd quickly come to appreciate her competence and loyalty in the short time he started working as head of Lee Holdings, there was something invigorating about having this fresh young face who brought the sensual scent of a woman to his office and offered him an eyeful of powerful sexuality.

It was easy to imagine her in his bed, to imagine his hands filled with her breasts, and her mouth filled with his...

"All done?" Zara called out as she popped back in the bathroom.

Leo cleared his throat and let go of his stiff, aching cock. Without even realizing it, he'd begun to stroke the hungry member. "Yeah." He punched the faucet shut and Zara flicked a warm towel over the shower door.

"I've hung a fresh suit on the back of the bathroom door," she said.

"Thank you." He stepped out with the large towel wrapped around his waist only to find she'd already left the bathroom. So much for his big, romantic plans with his new assistant.

He dried off and quickly walked back to his office when he heard his phone ring.

"I'm sorry," Zara said into the phone. "Mr. Lee just stepped out of the office for a moment. Would you like to leave a message?" As she jotted down the caller's name and number, she glanced up at Leo a few times, her smile a little hungrier every time. "I'll make sure he gets the message."

She hung up and came up to Leo with the message in hand. Blushing, she swallowed deeply and hesitated before speaking. "Do you need help getting dressed?" The message fluttered out of her hand and she fumbled to catch it in mid air. Failing, she stooped down to pick it up, but her jittery fingers seemed unable to accomplish the simple task.

"I've got it," Leo said as he quickly bent down and picked up the message. Reaching out for her hand, he helped her up. He was still wet from the shower, his chest dripped with droplets of water, and a towel slung low on his hips, exposing a V-line to one of the best-looking male bodies Zara had ever seen.

Zara stared at his tanned muscular chest and when she tripped over her three inch heels, she fell into his arms and brushed her fingers along his pecs.

Blushing profusely, she bit her lip and looked up at him.

Realizing what an embarrassing situation it might be for her, Leo said, "Maybe this'll be a little easier if you turn around for a minute." He spun her around and quickly pulled on his pants and shirt. No underwear. He went commando most of the time. "I think we're good now. I'm pretty decent." Heading to his desk, he flicked open the third drawer, pulled out a small blue box and extracted the diamond studded cufflinks he'd recently purchased.

In his periphery, he was aware of Zara's eyes on him, or maybe they were on the enormous diamonds that glittered in the rays of sun that now blazed through the other wall of windows.

"Now, I'm ready to face the day." He headed to the window to take in the spectacular view. "Thanks for your help, Zara ."

He barely had time to turn around when she threw herself on him and pushed him into the wall unit beside the window. As a rising star in action films, it wasn't the first time a female had thrown herself on him. Usually he kept his cool and would gently push them off before smiling and offering them an autograph, but with Zara, his body instantly reacted. Damn she smelled good, and felt good against him. Zara's body was firm and sumptuous, and his hands immediately found their way around her tiny little waist. Where had this gorgeous hot creature been hiding? It wasn't what he'd had in mind for that morning, but he was in no mood to fight it. He hadn't been with a woman since he first got back to Hong Kong.

The night before he left his house in Malibu, California in the U.S. for Hong Kong, he was enjoying the sensuous company of the coldly beautiful and very blonde Nicole Erikson, his co-star in his last film. Like the string of beautiful but detached models and actresses he would fuck hard and pleasured harder, Nicole was just one in many women who wanted only his body and some fun. He was a bad boy, a rebel against his family's expectations…he chose to be an actor, didn't he? He went away to the U.S. to get his college education at USC and then went into acting instead of returning home to Hong Kong. And he defied his father's choices of suitable potential wives for him from the "best" families in Hong Kong, although he was in his late 20s, and should be ready to settle down with a wife and family.

Instead, he chose to live his own life, instead of a life of a billionaire's son, and the path chosen for him. As he was thrusting into Nicole, clearly a woman his father wouldn't approve of with her piercings, tattoos, and penchant for kink; he was enjoying every minute of his chosen life until his phone started ringing. He was in the middle of climaxing with her when his phone first rang and kept ringing.

Without glancing at who was calling, as Nicole's head bobbed between his thighs, he grabbed his phone and tossed it into the next room.

It was only after his hot and sweaty sex-filled evening with Nicole, who left his house, looking bored and haughty, while smoking a cigarette, he checked his messages. That was when he found out his father had died. Worse, his father had tried to reach him by phone a few hours before, before he had taken his own life.

Guilt-ridden and in a mild depression following the news of his father's death, Leo threw himself into his new role as head of Lee Holdings, without any desire to date any woman or have sex with anyone for a long while. Until now. It had been a month after his father's death and tension had been building up in his body for too long.

"Hey," he whispered into her ear as she kept him pinned to the wall unit with her body. "How d'you know I liked it a little rough?" He wondered if Nicole had leaked about his sexual encounters with her, violating her confidentiality agreement with him. Being a public figure, he often had his encounters sign one.

"Huh?" She quickly turned around, pressing her ass into him as she glanced out the window.

His crotch heated up. "Oh, yeah. You definitely know what I like."

She was a bold little minx. The type of girl he could totally get into.

With her arms spread out, she prevented him from moving, but he still managed to thrust his pelvis forward, pressing his hardness into her cushy ass.

"Get down." Reaching back to grab his tie, she pulled him down and partially straddled him.

"You know, I'm used to playing the boss, but…"

"Shut up and stay still."

UNASSUMED

She was a domineering one. That was hot, and he wanted to play her game. "Baby, you've got to leave me some leeway." He reached around to grab her breast.

"Stop it," she hissed as she slapped his hand away. "I told you to stay still. They can sense motion and sound."

"Who's they? Is somebody watching us? I'm into that, babe. I've got an exhibitionist side."

"Hush." Zara silently crawled off him and, keeping her body pressed to the floor, passed beneath the windows and reached up to flick off the light switch.

"What the hell are you doing?" Leo whispered when she returned. "You like doing it in the dark?"

Ignoring him, she reached up to close the blinds.

"Will you tell me what the fuck is going on?"

"We've got to get out of here." She grabbed his hand. "Follow me."

He wasn't sure if it was all part of some wild game, and for a second he wanted to argue, but she tugged so hard on his arm that he relented and followed her into the small closet that housed his spare suits. Breathing hard, they stood face to face.

Now what, he thought as his hard-on made a comeback. He was eager to get into her pants and all she wanted to do was play silly games. With a mind of their own, his hands brushed up her arms and trickled down her back as he slowly pulled her to him.

"What do you think you're doing?" she spat.

"Hey, babe, I'm more confused than I've been in a long while. I haven't the faintest idea what I'm doing or what I'm supposed to be doing. You show up here this morning to tell me my assistant is no longer here, I don't know who the hell hired you, but damn, you're hot and I don't really care who made the decision. Then you undress me, and while I'm usually pretty good about remaining professional, it's hard to focus on business when a pretty girl is pulling my pants down. And now, all of a sudden, you go all weird and wacky on me."

"Mr. Lee. I have a confession to make."

"I'm ready for it."

"I am Detective Zara Zee."

She could have hit him in the gut and he wouldn't have been more shocked.

39

"Detective? What the hell is a detective doing here?"

With patient hands, she disentangled herself from his hold and backed up to the wall, putting a bit of space between them. "I'm with the Hong Kong Police Department. More precisely the OCUI; the Organized Crime Unit of Investigations."

"You know, I've had a lot of fans and groupies use very imaginative ways to get close to me over the years, but this takes the cake. Really… what are you doing here?"

"Mr. Lee, I'm sure you're already aware of the international crime ring that has taken hold of Hong Kong. They're powerful, they have the necessary funds and they don't hesitate to get rid of anyone who gets in their way. We have reason to believe, Mr. Lee, that you're getting in their way."

"That's ridiculous," he said with false bravado, but he knew better.

"I already know that you've been in contact with the French police. You were recently in Paris, were you not?"

"Yes."

"And you had the chance to see a few members of the French branch of this crime ring."

"Yes. They kidnapped my friend's future sister-in-law, Lilly Cooke."

"The daughter of Eugene Cooke who lost his company after millions were embezzled."

"How does all that relate to me?"

"You may not have heard, but during your absence from Hong Kong, the heir of The Lu Group was kidnapped."

He gasped. He'd been so preoccupied with everything that was going on in his life that he hadn't even checked the headlines of the paper, never mind the stories.

"The board of directors received a clear ransom demand from the kidnappers," she added. "Fifteen million dollars within forty-eight hours or they would kill him."

Leo let out a whistle. "Fifteen million? Were they able to get it?"

"Yes, but that didn't stop the ring from messing him up pretty bad. For reasons we still don't understand, they cut off all his toes, his ears, and...well, they killed him, and nearly caused his

41

building to topple. It was horrendous. Richard Lu died, and two officers on the case died while trying to rescue him."

"Ouch."

"They're not done. We think they're taunting us. For the past weeks, they've been staying just one step in front of us, and they know it."

"But how did all that bring us to hide out in my closet." He reached out to lay his hands on her hips, which fitted perfectly in his hands. "Not that I mind."

"The minute you stepped over to that window, I spotted a sniper in the building across the street. You were in his aim, Mr. Lee."

"Seriously?"

"Very seriously. You may not be aware of this, Mr. Lee, but they intended to kill Lilly Cooke. The only thing that stopped them was greed. They thought they could essentially make a slave of her and have her produce food for profit. In addition to their insatiable appetite for money and power, they are a dirty and unscrupulous band of criminals, and they are not to be taken lightly."

He squeezed the firm flesh that made her so sensually curvaceous. God, she felt good in his hands. "I promise to take it very seriously from now on."

"This is no laughing matter, Mr. Lee, and I take my job very seriously." She removed his hands from her hips and held them clasped in hers. "I'll be working undercover as your assistant until this is resolved, and don't doubt my professionalism for a minute. I will not let you out of my sight and I will do what I have to do to keep you safe."

"I'm obviously in good hands." The words were silky and sweet, but in the back of his mind, he had a million questions. What proof did he have that she was who she said she was? What if she was one of them? Part of the crime ring she claimed to want to keep him safe from? His years growing up as the heir to a billion dollars had taught him a lot about trust; namely, not to trust anyone. He'd fallen for pretenses more times than he could count, and he'd become wary of everyone.

Zara smiled. "I know you play an action hero in your movies, and I anticipated quite a bit of resistant from you. I'm happy to see you're ready to trust me."

"Just to be on the safe side..." He looked intently into her eyes.

She chuckled. "So, you don't trust me after all."

"You can never be too safe."

She pulled the fabric of her dress down to show him the sheer lace bra that highlighted her perfectly pert nipples. He grew harder, despite himself. Her body clearly wanted his, too.

"Hmm," he said with a hungry smile. "While I approve and would love to lose myself in... your endowment, that's not really the proof I was looking for."

"The badge clipped to my bra, sir... the badge," she said in an annoyed tone.

Licking his lips, he imagined putting his head between the two mounds of soft, firm flesh. He was hungry... so horny. He wanted her so badly, he could almost taste her. Her breasts were perfect.

"Are you satisfied, Mr. Lee?"

He cleared his throat. "For now." Keeping control of his urges would be difficult if she continued to dress so provocatively. Trying to shake off the sensual images he had of her, he reminded himself of her profession. She was an officer of the law and he had to respect that.

She glared at him.

"Yes. I'm satisfied."

"Good. I'm going to open the closet door now. Don't move." She cracked the door open, scanned the office and looked out the window. "Looks like he left, but we'll have to be on our guard."

"Who's to say he won't come back?"

She huffed with impatience and walked back into the darkened office. "Get on with your day, Mr. Lee and act as normally as you can… go out to lunch, go to the gym… do whatever it is that the hot, young heir of Lee Holdings does in a typical day."

"Hot?"

"I beg your pardon."

"You said I was hot. It's a little surprising coming from you."

She smiled and suddenly the naïve and clueless sweet girl she'd initially shown herself to be returned. "Did I really say that?" Playfully biting the tip of her little finger, she gazed up at him. She looked like a vulnerable and shy nineteen year old now instead of the what, twentysomething experienced and older detective that she was. She was like some male fantasy come true. A real detective, who was sexy and beautiful at the same time.

The bulge in his pants quickly returned and he wondered how long he'd be able to hold back. She was making it impossible. "It's flattering to know you think I'm hot." As she turned her attention to the pile of folders on his desk, he came up behind her and whispered in her ear, "Especially since I find you so scorching hot. With all due respect, officer, I can't help imagining all the things I would love to do to you."

With a tantalizing smile on her lips, she looked over her shoulder at him, the invitation so clear in her eyes.

She looked delicious.

Then she said, "Sorry, I don't get involve with my subjects."

Leo was confused and blinked his eyes before asking, "Subject?"

"Yes, you're the subject I'm protecting. The target. I'm sorry, but I can't get involved. You know...like a doctor and his patient. I can't, for personal reasons."

Leo let out a big breath and ran his fingers through his hair. "Well, if I'm just a subject to you, then, I'm sorry too. I thought there was chemistry between us, but I guess wrong. I'll stay out of your hair then."

He walked out of his office without a second glance at her, and when he left, Zara felt the room suddenly grow colder.

Chapter 3

Zara

Fitting in at Leopold's office wasn't much of a problem for Zara. She'd always had a knack for staying under the radar when it came to undercover work and this billionaire's workplace was no different.

With her long dark hair pulled up into a sleek ponytail, a decent amount of make up and the right clothes, no one would ever think she was anything other than the boss's assistant.

That morning she'd pulled on a grey version of the same skirt she'd worn the day before. Accustomed to wearing a uniform when she'd been a police officer and then moving on to comfortable slacks and a plain blue button down shirt when she'd first made detective, dressing up and fussing with hair and make up was relatively new to her, but it was something she enjoyed. The impossibly high heels were a welcomed change from the sturdy black shoes with well treaded soles she usually wore. She enjoyed wearing that red dress in her closet for her first day at Lee Holdings, although it was more of an evening date type of dress. She didn't care. It was a chance to get dressed up, while making an impression on Mr. Leopold Lee. She wasn't just any assistant who was stepping in for Mrs. Huang, but she was a bold and strong woman who could tear off the arms of any man who dared laid a hand on her, too.

"Leo's looking for you," Hannah said as she walked into the photocopying room.

Well, I've been looking for him, Zara wanted to say. He'd disappeared without a word right after lunch and her repeated attempts to call him had been in vain.

"Thanks." She quickly picked up the documents she'd been photocopying and headed back to her office to call him. "Leo," she said when he picked up.

The sound of dozens of voices around him murmured into her phone.

"Where are you?" she nearly shouted. "You ran out on me after lunch."

"My apologies. It wasn't intentional. I'm at the Oyster House. I need you here… now."

"Is everything all right? Did something happen?"

"Everything is great. Just get down here."

She looked at the stack of photocopies on her desk and patted it affectionately. "I just made copies of some of your employee profiles. I'd hoped to have a chance to look through them. Maybe I could find a disgruntled Lee Holdings employee or ex-employee who has it in for you."

"Good to know you're a diligent worker, but I need you here. You can check the profiles later."

Biting her bottom lip, she nodded. "Fine. I'll be right there."

She hung up and stashed her precious photocopies in the bottom drawer of her desk and locked it. Grabbing her purse and blazer, she walked out of the office, locking it behind her.

"Already off for the afternoon," Hannah, the receptionist said as she whizzed by.

"Duty calls." She hopped into the first elevator and rode down to the underground parking garage. As

Leo's assistant her reserved parking space was nearby, right beside Leo's.

The streets from the office to the restaurant were congested and after twenty minutes she took matters into her own hands. Pulling out the magnetic portable siren and light, she affixed it to the roof of the car and flicked it on. Within seconds she was driving through the streets at a reasonable speed as drivers cleared the way for her. Although she hated to abuse such power, she told herself that Leo could very well be in danger and simply wasn't in a position to state it.

In just under ten minutes she arrived at the Oyster House and hurried inside. The moment she entered the swank and hip restaurant, she knew there was no emergency, at least not of the legal kind.

Though the place was full, it was surprisingly quiet and somber. White tablecloths were draped over each table, topped with soft pink linen napkins and beautiful bouquets of pink and white flowers. Exquisite flatware sparkled against fine china as the quiet patrons nibbled delicate morsels of gourmet food.

At the kitchen door, speaking to two waitresses, Leo stood with his hands deep in his pockets. Beyond him was a flurry of activity as tray after tray emerged on the hand of yet another waitress. Frowning, he was clearly upset and unhappy about something. His gaze flicked around the room and came to rest on Zara . A tight smile curved his lips as he dismissed his employees and waved her over.

Zara meandered through the tables and came to him. "This is quite a crowd. What's the special occasion?"

"It's a charity fundraiser benefiting Hong Kong's Hospital for Women."

"Oh. I've heard of that. They do great work."

"Absolutely."

"What did you call me here for? What do you need me to do?"

"You're my assistant, right? My assistant should be here at a time like this."

"Right."

"Besides, I have a speech to make in about ten minutes." He reached into his breast pocket and pulled out a few sheets of neatly folded paper. "I'd like you to take a look at it."

She took the sheets. "You do realize that I'm a detective and not a proofreader."

He shrugged as he headed to the back office. "I just want you to see if everything makes sense and if it's sensitive enough. You know... a woman's perspective."

She wanted to argue that it wasn't truly a part of her job, but quickly realized it was for a good cause.

"You're a little loquacious, aren't you?" she said as she unfolded the wordy pages.

"Only when I have something to say."

"Fair enough." Zara leaned her butt back against the edge of Leo's desk and read the first page. As she began the second page, tears came to her eyes and she tried desperately to keep them in check, but by the end of the third page, she had to stop."

"This is beautiful," she blubbered.

"I was hoping you'd be moved."

"Mr. Lee," a perky young employee said as she poked her head inside the office. "They're ready for you."

"I'll be right there." He reached out for his speech, his trembling hand betraying him.

"Nervous?" Zara said with an affectionate smile. "I never would have thought a big star like you would fear public speaking."

"It's not speaking in public I'm worried about. It's the story."

She patted his shoulder. "It's a very touching story. I'm sure they'll all appreciate you sharing it with them."

His eyes locked with hers. The tension in his jaw dissipated and his dark brown eyes softened. A wan smile came to his lips for a fleeting moment as he reached for her hand. "Thank you. I think I needed that."

They walked back into the quiet restaurant and Leo made his way to a small stage erected for the occasion.

"*Nin hao ma*. Good afternoon, everyone and thank you for coming," he said when all eyes turned to him. "I'm sure some of you have never given much thought to Hong Kong's Hospital for Women. I would say you're very fortunate if you've never had to walk through their doors. You have true wealth; your health. But I'm sure that many of you know precisely what happens beyond those doors. Many of you have been tested, diagnosed and treated at this very special hospital. Many more of you have visited patients there; patients who were treated with care and respect.

But some of you are probably wondering what all this has to do with me, an action film star with culinary aspirations. Well, let me tell you.

"When I was a young boy, a very dear woman fell ill. Doctors said it was ovarian cancer, advanced ovarian cancer; untreatable, incurable, and unforgiving. She had nowhere to go other than family, and while her family, her children, her siblings and her friends did their best to make her comfortable, the pain intensified and the strain quickly overwhelmed everyone.

"When her children last saw her, she was frail and thin, and while her smile was stoic, they knew she was in unimaginable pain. Had the hospital existed then, things could have been different for her.

"Two years following her death, her daughter was diagnosed with the very same cancer, but that's where the similarity ends. The women's hospital had just opened their doors and she was one of their very first patients. Treatment was efficient, quick, and administered with love and care, and within the year, she was given a clean bill of health."

Leo swallowed and his eyes grew misty. For a moment he seemed unable to continue, but he cleared his throat, blinked away the intense emotions and looked at the crowd that hung on his every word. "I would not be standing here today if it wasn't for Hong Kong's Hospital for Women. You see, the older woman who died so many years ago was my grandmother, a woman I never met, never knew, and the woman who was saved by the efficient treatment given at the hospital was my mother. She was pregnant with me when she got the diagnosis. I shouldn't be standing here in front of you today. At least that's what many people told her at the time; that she should terminate the pregnancy, that her health was too frail.

"As you prepare to open your purses, your wallets, and your checkbooks, please be generous, for your mothers, your sisters, your daughters and for every other woman who has ever touched your lives. I am proud to be the first to place in this basket a check for two million dollars. The hospital needs you, needs us. Equipment is expensive, treatment is expensive, and talented doctors, nurses and lab technicians are expensive. On behalf of all women, I thank you. *Xie xie nin de bang zhu.*"

A gentle and reverent spattering of applause filled the room and the moment Leo stepped down, he was surrounded by women eager to thank him and share their own stories. Through it all, he was charming and compassionate and emerged profoundly touched by the response.

"I'm glad you asked me to come be here," Zara said when he'd finally disengaged himself. "I wouldn't have wanted to miss such a poignant and touching moment. I've already made a check to the hospital. It's not quite as generous as yours, but…"

"Every bit helps. While a few people are in a position to make large donations, most make very modest donations, but they add up. Come," he said as he took a gentle hold of her forearm. "I have a few people I'd like to introduce you to."

She'd never felt particularly comfortable amidst high society and as Leo introduced her to Hong Kong's elite, she felt the scrutinizing gaze of the women drill through her. She smiled and shook their hands, but sensed their disdain.

Flustered and eager to break away as the women returned to their conversation, Zara glanced at the doors that led out to the terrace.

"Let's get you some air," Leo said as he guided her out. "You okay?"

"Yes, I'm fine." Frowning, she set her hands on the rail and looked out at the harbor. It was a beautiful afternoon, and the clear skies allowed a perfect view of Lee Holdings clear on the other side.

"Then you need to tell it to your face, because you don't look fine." Leo came up and set his hands beside hers, his left hand almost brushing against her right. "You looked more and more uncomfortable with every passing minute back there. Did I miss something? Did something happen?"

Zara shrugged. "I guess hobnobbing with high society isn't really my thing."

He cocked his head to the side. "Oh. Did someone here say anything to make you feel... inferior?"

"No," she gasped. "Of course not." At least not outright. "Some of them looked at me kind of funny. Like I was from another world."

Leo looked her up and down. "You know, Zara that skirt fits you like a glove and your shirt is perfectly pressed."

She ran her hands over her hips. "Thank you."

"It's a great professional look."

"Thank you."

"But it's a little too tame for the Oyster House, and it may be a little too... secretarial for a fundraising luncheon."

Indignant, she lifted her chin. "First of all, I wasn't aware I was coming to a luncheon, and secondly, I'm here as your assistant, Leo. I can't very well wear..." Her gaze wandered to the group of sexy young socialites sitting at a table just beyond the French doors. Their assets were well in view, and one particularly well-endowed woman wore a dress worthy of a high end brothel.

"We're not at the office anymore. I want you to fit in. It's bad enough I have to have you following me everywhere as your 'subject'... some poor hapless victim who can't protect himself and requires a petite woman like yourself to protect me. It doesn't matter that I've made a name for myself as an action figure and martial artist. If you are going to follow me, you could make an effort to make it a more enjoyable experience."

"I'll make note of that and try to do better. As for following you around, it's just a precaution, one that I think you should take more seriously. Leaving the office without telling me where you're going is negligent on your part.

"I know, and I've apologized for that."

"If you think I'm cramping your style, Mr. Lee, just imagine what being kidnapped and held at gunpoint will do to your lifestyle. Having me around is a small price to pay for your freedom. Considering what happened to this crime ring's most recent billionaire victim, I'd think you'd be more than happy to have me around." Zara's gaze remained on the young socialites and couldn't fathom dressing like them.

Leo followed her gaze and grinned. "I am happy to have you around, and..." He directed her gaze to his face. "I don't expect you to dress like a slut, but I do want you to look hot and sexy."

"Aren't they one and the same?"

Chuckling, he guided her to a fancifully carved bench and sat down. "You have so much to learn."

"I beg your pardon." She didn't like his tone, or his insinuation. "Are you saying that I'm naïve?"

He shook his head. "Maybe you just work a little too much. When was the last time you took a vacation?"

Huffing with indignation, she tilted her face up to look at a colorful bird perched high in the nearby tree. "Last spring we were invited to a week long training session in Sanya. We were there five days and four nights."

"That's hardly a vacation."

"Have you ever been to Sanya? It's a very relaxing setting."

"I'm sure it is, but I'm thinking more along the lines of a weekend in Paris, or a week in Bora Bora, or two weeks in Dubai."

She waved the notion away. "I'm not interested in that." She turned to look pointedly at him. "You know, the thing is that I really do love my job. When you love what you do, every day is a vacation. When people take a vacation it's to get away from a job they don't enjoy. It's to break away from the monotony, to put some spice in their life. My days are far from monotonous, and, believe me, I don't need any added spice. My life is spicy enough as it is."

UNASSUMED

"What are you afraid of, Zara? Spending too much time with yourself?"

"Why won't anyone believe me? I really do love my job."

"No matter how much you love your job, everyone needs time away every once in a while. I would think in your line of work, that time away would be crucial."

"Well, you'd be wrong."

He laughed. "It wouldn't be the first time." Looking at her, he ran his finger along her fine cheek bones and down the cut of her jaw. "You have the face of an angel and the body of a lingerie model. What made you want to become a detective of all things?"

She stood suddenly and paced in front of him.

"Sit back down." Leo took her hand and pulled her back to his side. His eyes darkened with concern. "What'd I say to agitate you so?"

Running her hand over her face, she struggled to find the words to tell him. It wasn't the first time she'd been asked the question. It'd come up when she'd first enrolled in the academy, then again when she'd graduated, and yet again when she'd made detective. Every time she'd given a flippant remark about idolizing various television detectives.

So why was it now so impossible to give Leo that simple explanation?

"What happened?" he said.

"When I was a little girl, we lived just outside of Shantou. We didn't have much, but I was a happy child. I loved the country, loved the fresh air and loved the outdoors."

"Sounds like an idyllic childhood."

"It could have been," she said in a mournful groan. "It should have been."

"What changed it?"

"My parents died when I was a child. Some kind of accident that I was too young to understand. I was sent to live with my grandmother, who was strict and old-fashioned. I didn't grow up with much of the modern conveniences everyone did. Grandma didn't even own a television. She owned a bike, not some fancy car, and she made me walk everywhere. Instead of lessons in piano or horseback riding like some of your friends in there, I spent all my free time hitting blocks of wood, sparring, learning how to kick and punch. Grandma didn't care that I was a girl. She said

63

that because I was a girl, I had to work harder, be tougher, and strive further. Because I was the youngest of the Zee's and my family's only child, I had to stay focus on my family legacy."

"Oh," Leo groaned. "Family legacy…I know how that feels."

"I remembered my father was a decent and honorable man, one who didn't care if his own safety was at stake. He worked hard to support us, while mother taught at a local school. I don't remember what happened, but Grandma was very sad and angry after she found out about their accident. The police said it was just an accident, but growing up, Grandma often told me there was more to it. She refused to believe my father was under the influence, highly intoxicated with alcohol when he crashed."

"What made her think that?" Leo asked.

"Well, for one thing, Grandma said that it couldn't be. My father didn't drink. He was highly allergic to alcohol. He would never knowingly touch the stuff. Let alone go driving with my mother in the car after getting drunk."

64

"People who drink can't control themselves, Zara," Leo said, looking sheepish. "You witnessed how I behaved the day after. I wasn't exactly a gentleman, which I apologize for, by-the-way, Officer," Leo said, with a smile.

God, he was intensely adorable at that moment, which Zara reminded herself, was why he was considered one of the most handsome and desirable men in Hong Kong. He was also her responsibility, she told herself, tearing her eyes away from his.

Haunted tears filled her eyes, blurring the vision of her tortured father and dying mother.

"Well, I was only five at the time, and I believe Grandma. My parents' deaths weren't just an accident. I swore I'd find the men who'd killed my parents. I would do the job the police had been unable to do."

"That's quite a motivation. So you became a cop."

With a crooked smile, she looked at him through the tears. "Oh, I've had plenty of motivation in my life. Living with Grandma in Kowloon City, and not the pleasant section of town, opened my eyes to the world real quick," she said with a sarcastic smirk.

UNASSUMED

"Every little errand I made for her was like walking through a war zone. I got pushed around for being a little kid. I got robbed when I had just enough change in my hand to buy a piece of fish. And when I got older, when my body attracted a different kind of attention, I was harassed by men of all ages. I was sick of it. I was tired of being small, and frail and weak. I learned martial arts."

She shrugged and laughed. "I tried learning it on my own...just moves I've seen in old kung fu films without really knowing what I was doing until a friend of my grandmother's who often came around to help her out saw me one day. Initially he just laughed and dismissed the notion that such a small frail girl could ever learn anything about martial arts, but after a while he started showing me various techniques, and when he saw how serious I was and how quickly I learned, he intensified the lessons. Uncle Chang; that's what I used to call him. He looked like any old man selling ancient Chinese herbs down at his herb shop, but he had been a kung fu champion back when he was a young man. I learned a lot from him, but he said that I could learn more...go up another level of mastery, and guess who could teach me."

"Who?" Leo asked.

"My grandmother," Zara said. "Turns out he and Uncle Chang were classmates, taught by my great grandfather himself. And he was taught by his grandfather and so on in a long tradition that went all the way back to the Qi Dynasty, and originated with the Prince of Lan Ling, Gao Su."

"The Prince of Lan Ling?" Leo asked. "The legendary brave and handsome prince of China back in the 6th Century A.D."

"My ancestor was close to the Prince, and some say the prince really didn't die of poisoning from his own brother, but had pretended to die. That although the Gao dynasty was wiped out, the Prince survived and had descendants. I really don't know much about all that, but it's nice to know something about my parents and family ancestry. It was something Grandma was proud of, although it doesn't help us out today. Nonetheless, Grandma provided more training beyond Uncle Chang's. She told me that I was my father's daughter, and a Zee. I had to learn to be the best in martial arts. I came from a long line of martial artists, many serving as the imperial guards of royal families. Grandma was proud of that heritage, and although she hardly spoke of her past, she hinted at a much more glamorous life when she was younger."

"Does that mean I need to be careful around you?" Leo asked.

Tilting her head down, she looked sidelong at him. "I could give you a serious run for your money, Mr. Movie Star. It means you don't have to feel like your ego is bruised having a girl like me protect you. I'm not just any girl, you know."

"I know," Leo said in a deep guttural voice that made Zara blushed. It sounded like a sensual caress against her skin. "I'm up for the challenge."

Smiling, she lifted her head and looked up at the late afternoon sky. She'd never told anyone the story of her childhood and felt the heavy burden of her parents' death lifted from her shoulders.

Leo stood to face her, his eyes intent on her face. "You're quite an impressive woman. You almost make me feel silly and insignificant for having learned martial arts simply to be in the movies."

"Hey, we all have our paths in life." She smirked. "I won't hold against you the fact that you lived in a gilded castle with a silver spoon in your mouth."

"I might have been coddled, but that didn't keep me from going out there and working hard to become who I am today. I know plenty of young men who've inherited from their fathers and they just sit back and take it easy. I put in six hours of training every day to master martial arts, and I had plenty of rejection from the movie industry before I was finally taken seriously."

"And now you're hoping the culinary world will take you seriously as well."

"What's life if you don't have the ambition to move forward?"

Zara smiled and felt more at ease than she had in a long time. It wasn't quite what she'd expected from him. She'd heard he could be difficult, and she'd thought she'd be protecting a brat. She'd also heard he could be a diva, and she'd anticipated a slew of unreasonable demands.

"You're a pleasant surprise," she blurted out, quickly regretting her words.

"Really?" he said with interest. "What surprises you? That I enjoy cooking? That I don't use my martial arts ability every chance I get? That I'm not using my celebrity status to impress you?"

Laughing, she pulled away from him. "All of the above."

Amusement sizzled in his eyes as he closed in on her and tapped his forehead to hers. "And you haven't even seen my rebellious side yet," he whispered.

As they walked back into the restaurant, Leo was quickly surrounded by women of all ages. Some wanted to thank him before they left, others wanted a word with him about the money being raised, and many wanted more, much more. Leo took it all in stride, and Zara enjoyed watching him in his element. He had a charming and endearing way about him, and she now understood why he had such a strong female fan base.

But as charming as he was, it didn't stop her from keeping a critical eye on the crowd at large. While the women were surely all sincere in their desire to speak to Leo, Zara had to remain on the lookout for any attempt at foul play.

In the far corner she saw them; two men in dark suits speaking to one another with their heads low. In a room filled with flowing pastels, shimmering satins and fashionable florals, they stood out and were instantly conspicuous. Ready for a confrontation, she slowly, but surely made her way to the whispering men.

As she approached, she saw that one of them was a young man, perhaps twenty-five, with a thin mustache and spiked hair, while the other man, shorter and significantly older, had silver grey hair a clean shaven face and a diamond stud earring in one ear.

Zara 's heart pounded as it always did when she sensed she was onto something. The adrenaline, the thrill, the excitement… and the satisfaction of nabbing another criminal; they all pushed her on, urging her to put a stop to whatever plans they might have.

She stopped at the table set with three large bouquets of flowers and pamphlets regarding the women's hospital. With her back to the suspicious men, she perused an article that had appeared in the local paper. It praised not only the hospital, but Leopold Lee's part in the fundraising.

"I don't know," the younger man said. "Couldn't we wait until evening to make our move?"

"No," the older man said with assurance. "We need to do this now so he knows we mean business."

"Look around this place," the younger one said. "There are people everywhere. Someone's bound to see or hear something."

"That's where you're wrong. There are a lot of people here and that is exactly what's going to make this easier. No one will notice he's gone. No one will miss him. It'll be hours before they realize what happened."

Zara made her move, and quickly cornered the men, handcuffing them before they act. "You're not doing anything, gentlemen."

"Hey," the older one groaned. "What's going on?"

"Let's quietly head to the kitchen and we'll let the police handle this."

Chapter 4

Leo

The head chef's eyes practically popped out when he saw Zara lead the two men into the kitchen. His lips parted and his brow furrowed, but he remained silent, though clearly unhappy with the situation.

The two men looked up at the chef. "Hey, Eddie," the young man said.

"Jack? Rob? How d'you...? What are you guys doing here?" Eddie said, his eyes wide with surprise and a hint of fear.

"We heard you were back in town. Imagine our surprise. We thought you'd left Hong Kong for good. It's been so long since we last saw you, we thought we'd pop in and visit you."

"Right. Right," Zara said. "Nice try guys. I suggest you remain quiet until the police gets here."

"Police?" Eddie said. "What's the police have to do with this?"

"These men were plotting something, and I thwarted their plans."

"Thwarted our plans to surprise an old buddy, here," Rob said drily.

"Hey," Craig said. "How d'you end up with this gig anyway? I thought you were through with Hong Kong after our last... transaction? Last time I saw you, you had your tail between your legs."

Eddie laughed, but it was a nervous and uncomfortable sound. "Long story short, I ran into Leo Lee on the set of a movie a while back, he introduced me to the famed French chef, Errol King, who trained me, taught me everything I know, and now, here I am."

"Oh, brother," Zara groaned, eager to have the police show up. Where were they anyway?

"Looks like a really nice place," Rob said with a scrutinizing gaze around the well equipped kitchen. "Looks like you'll have a real hit on your hands."

"Guys, I know I shouldn't have run out like that, but... Look, this place is legit, and Leo is a real good guy who worked hard to open this place. Leave the restaurant out of this. It's a classy joint and we don't want any trouble here."

"You should've thought of that when you ran away," Craig said.

"We don't want any trouble either, Eddie," Rob said in a calm, soothing tone. "Give us what we came here for, and you'll never see us in this place again, unless it's for a nice dinner. Man, it smells good in this place."

"That's enough, guys," Zara said, shaking both their handcuffs to quiet them down.

"You've got nothing on us, sweetheart," Rob said with a glance over his shoulder at her.

"I heard threats. And it's detective, not sweetheart."

Rob chuckled and seemed not the least bit intimidated by her.

"Threats? What did we threaten? To surprise him? To take him away for a few hours to talk this thing out?"

Leo pushed through the swinging double doors and took a quick sweep of the situation. "What the hell is going on here?" His gaze quickly left the men's face and settled on Zara's.

"These men didn't come to the Oyster House to participate in the fundraiser. They were acting suspicious and I overheard them making plans to take someone away. My colleagues should be here any minute to take them into custody for a few questions."

"Call them off this minute. I don't need the police coming around here."

"But they…"

"Please, Zara ," he snapped. "Call them off!"

Taking a step back, Zara pulled out her phone and quietly cancelled her request.

"Done," she said in a flat tone when she stepped forward once again. Unhappy with the way Leo had spoken to her, she glared at him, but he didn't seem to notice.

Eddie backed away and cast his gaze to the floor.

"Does this have anything to do with you, Eddie?" Leo said.

"I swear. I didn't know they were coming." He looked directly at Rob and Craig. "We could have discussed this at another time… another place."

"They're here now," Leo said, clearly annoyed by the distraction. "What is this all about?"

"I owe them a bit of money."

"How much?"

"A lot more than a bit," Rob said.

"How much?" Leo repeated.

"About fifty grand."

"You're closing in on seventy-five with the interest."

Leo's jaw tightened as he digested the information. He glared at Eddie, Rob and Craig, and back at Eddie. "I really don't like to meddle in other people's affairs, and if you owe these guys money, I'm tempted to let them do to you whatever they feel is right."

Zara gasped, but said nothing.

"But I can't afford to let them take you away..." He glanced at the loan sharks. "... and break whatever limb they need to break to teach you a lesson. Thing is, I need you here. So, I'll tell you what I'm going to do. I'll pay this debt..."

"Oh, my God. Thank you. You're an incredibly kind and understanding man, boss. I can't begin to tell you how much I appreciate this."

"Don't be so quick to thank me. I try every day to be a kind and understanding man, and a fair boss, but don't think for a minute that you can take advantage of that. I'll dock you a significant amount

from your paycheck every week until the debt is paid."
He turned once again to Rob and Craig. "We got a
deal?"

"You've got yourself a deal, Mr. Lee."

"You," Leo said to Eddie, "get back to work."

"Yes, sir. I won't let you down." Eddie went
back to work.

"Bring them back to my office," Leo instructed
Zara.

A little flustered, she did as she was told.

"You can remove the cuffs," Leo said once in
his office.

Clenching her jaw, she removed the handcuffs.
"I hope you know what you're doing," she said. "The
least you should do is let the police question them…
make sure they're…"

"I'll pay the debt, keep them out of the police's
hands and they'll steer clear of my establishment." He
looked pointedly at the men.

"Absolutely," Rob said.

His jaw tight and his eyes dark, Leo pulled a
checkbook out of the top drawer of his desk and
flicked it open. "Seventy-five thousand you said,
right?"

"Sorry," Craig said. "We'll need cash. Although, if you could give me an autograph, my kid would be thrilled."

Leo snorted his annoyance as he slapped the checkbook atop his desk. "I'll get you the cash." He headed for the door. "I'll be right back."

Crossing her arms over her chest, Zara kept a close eye on the men as they waited for Leo to return.

"You're pretty hot for a detective," Craig said, looking at her. "You could probably make a lot more money as a…"

"I make enough, thank you," she snapped.

Leo returned with a thick envelope in hand. "Here you go." He slapped the envelope into Craig's chest. "Now get out of here before anyone gets wind of this."

"No problem."

Leo looked at Zara. "Would you mind escorting them to the back entrance? There are reporters all over the place. I don't need this kind of publicity."

"Sure thing."

With a hand to their elbows, Zara guided the men to the discreet back entrance. "You guys got lucky. If I ever hear that you guys came back for more, I won't hesitate to book you."

Craig winked, and Rob gave her a cocky salute before heading out.

Zara returned to Leo's office and quietly closed the door behind her.

"Ah," he said with an amused sigh. "My little detective vixen. No sooner do I turn my back do you go on the prowl for a criminal."

She smirked back at him, happy to see he could find humor in such a situation. He clearly had a good head on his shoulders and knew how to keep his cool in a confrontation.

He sauntered up to her, his gaze appraising as his dark, smoldering eyes took her in. "I have to admit, having you is getting pretty interesting."

Chapter 5

Zara

At five thirty the next morning, Zara was already up and in the shower. She enjoyed taking her time in the morning; a long shower, a few cups of strong coffee and a glimpse at the morning news. It was a ritual she'd started while at the academy and it remained with her still. It was a zen moment that got her day off to a good start. It also helped her transition into the undercover cop/assistant at Lee Holdings better. It had been three weeks now since she first started, and although she and Leo still acted formally with each other at the office, they had settled into a comfortable situation at his penthouse where he was living. Being an undercover cop to ensure his safety, she stayed with him at his penthouse, keeping guard at night, while sleeping on the sofa. It was a nice situation for her, since his penthouse suite was luxurious beyond anything she's lived in, but it took getting used to in the beginning for both of them. So whenever they could, they would try to be independent and separate from each other. She dried off with her thick, fluffy towel, her phone emitted the gentle tinkling sound that signaled a text. Clicking it on, she brought up the text.

Never mind the office this morning. Meet me at the Aesop Fashion Walk in front of DKNY.

Zara frowned as she read the message a third time. Why in the world did he want her to meet him there? And how was she expected to dress this time? In shorts and a tank top? A flowery summer dress? Jeans and a t-shirt?

Aesop Fashion Walk. She'd never even dared go to the area. Most of her shopping was done in discount stores with the occasional foray to a semi-chic boutique.

She finally opted for a pair of dark skinny jeans and a simple black button down shirt. Hoping to add a bit of oomph to her simple outfit, she slipped into a pair of comfy three inch black heels.

After a good breakfast and her third cup of coffee, she got her things together and headed out the door. Being up early had its advantages. Traffic was light as she left her apartment in Sha Tin and headed to

Fashion Walk, but once there she ended up pacing in front of the designer shop for over an hour before Leo arrived.

He pulled his black Porsche up the curb and stepped out wearing casual black slacks and a relaxed white shirt that was flattering in its simplicity. With black shades and his hair sleeked back, he was the epitome of cool, so cool, just looking at him shot a chill up Zara 's spine.

"So what did you call me down here for?" she said, desperate to camouflage the effect he had on her.

He pulled his shades down just enough to wink at her before slipping them back up the bridge of his nose. "Please don't think I'm wearing these because I'm full of myself," he said. "It's just a feeble attempt at going a little incognito this morning."

"I wouldn't dare think that of you."

"Is that a bit of sarcasm I hear in your voice?"

"A bit?" she threw back with a playful grin.

"So," he said with a clap of his hands. "What did I call you down here for? Well, for a little bit of shopping of course. So why don't we start right here at DKNY."

UNASSUMED

Her heart suddenly beat ferociously, and the moment they stepped inside the designer shop, she felt out of place. Everything was so beautiful; the colors, the textures, the patterns... even the scent.

"I'm going to need you to try on a few dresses."

"Me? Why?"

Leo looked her up and down. "You seem to be about the same size as this girl I'm dating, and I want to surprise her with a nice summer wardrobe. I want her to have a few frilly summer dresses, some classic cocktail dress and a few formal gowns."

At the mention of another woman, an odd pang of discomfort quickly lodged itself in the core of Zara's being, and she couldn't for the life of her understand why. Leo was a client, a man she'd been hired to protect. A man she knew very little about. What he did with his personal life was none of her concern, and if he had a female friend...

Argh!

If she was such a professional, with a professional relationship with her client, why was the image of him with another woman so disturbing?

Leo didn't seem to notice her discomfort at all. With the help of a clerk, he picked out a few dresses. "A simple black dress, a black and white cocktail dress and a white lace summer dress. Let's start with that."

Feeling like a little girl who'd been given free reign of a candy store, Zara headed into a dressing room and tried on the three dresses. After each one, she came out to show Leo the results.

"Perfect," he said time and again. Pleased with the three dresses, he paid and they were once again out on the streets of Fashion Walk.

They went on to Max Mara where they picked up a teal cotton jacquard princess dress, then crossed the way to choose a few sizzling pieces of jewelry at Swarovski. After that, it was on to Vivienne Tam's for an exciting black and white floral cut out sleeveless top with matching skirt and then a quick stop at Alexandre de Paris for an onyx and tortoise ribbon hair clip and a romantic floral headband. Just when she thought she couldn't shop anymore, they stopped at Choi Fung Hong for a few cosmetics.

"This is all great," Leo said. "But I think we need something with even a little more... oomph." He led her back to his car where they filled the small trunk with the morning's purchases. "Off to Valentino's," he said as he put the car in gear. "And maybe even a stop at DeBeer's."

He took Queen's road and stopped at Valentino's couture house. The moment they entered, Zara's eyes were immediately drawn to a magnificent lambskin purse with the prominent "V" beside the golden clasp.

"This is so darling," she said to the clerk. "How much is it?"

The clerk eyed Leo a second. "Three thousand, seven hundred dollars."

Zara gasped and set the purse back down, but Leo picked it up and handed it back to her.

"Now we need to find the perfect dress to go along with it."

The clerk quickly returned with a sleeveless crew neck cocktail dress. "This is embroidered linen embellished with tiny beads. The fit is sublime."

Zara marveled at the dress. It was spectacular to say the least, and so was the nearly ten thousand dollar price tag. As she slipped into the dress, she couldn't help but envy the girl who was to receive such a lavish wardrobe.

"My car didn't even cost this much," she muttered to herself as she looked at her reflection. "Is this what it looks like to be a socialite?" For a moment, she allowed herself the fantasy; a life of leisure, a life filled with the best things in life. A life with Leo in it.

Shaking the useless fantasy away, she emerged from the fitting room and slid her hands into the ample pockets. "It even has pockets," she told Leo with a chuckle.

"We'll take it," he simply said to the clerk as she came around with another garment.

Once again, Zara disappeared into the fitting room and quickly returned.

"Each dress is more fabulous than the last." He nodded at the clerk who took note of another purchase.

"Anything else?" Zara said.

"We can't leave Valentino's without an exquisite gown or two."

No sooner had he finished his statement than the clerk hung a floor length nude gown trimmed in gold in the fitting room. The long puffy sleeves and ample skirt were elegant and ultra-feminine, while the transparency of the fabric lent a touch of subtle sensuality.

UNASSUMED

As she looked at her reflection from every angle, the clerk slipped a pair of printed calfskin sandals under the door.

It was all so painfully perfect. She never wanted to take the garment off.

"Can we have a look?" Leo called out after a while.

She stepped out feeling like a princess from head to toe, but apparently the clerk wasn't completely satisfied with the look. Coming up behind Zara, she pulled her long hair up, gave it a twist and pinned it into place.

"Ravishing. You look like a goddess," Leo whispered in awe. He looked at the clerk. "Order that one as well. It's positively perfect. I already know the event I'll want her to wear it to."

Zara pressed her lips together, anything to hide how upsetting it was to hear him talk of time with this other girl.

"And our next stop; Barney Cheng."

Zara had heard of the designer and had seen a few of his gowns in a magazine; the type of garments she'd never even dreamed of.

By the time they'd walked out of his shop, Leo had ordered a black and coral qipao, a blue chiffon gown and a fuchsia satin gown with capelet.

"This all makes for an elaborate wardrobe," Zara said.

"I like to know the girl on my arm will be dressed for the part. I'm often photographed at public events, not to mention movie premieres. She has to be ultrachic and glamorous. Her appearance will be noted, judged and picked apart. I won't have my girl on the worst dressed list. No way." He slipped her hand into the crook of his arm. "And now we need a little va-va-voom. Come on."

They entered another boutique where Leo quickly went to a vivid red one-sleeved dress. "Is this va-va-voom enough?"

"It certainly appears to be," Zara said as she entered the fitting room. The asymmetrical red dress had a splash of white flowers running diagonally from one shoulder to the opposing hemline. It was fresh and sexy, and when she swiped her lips with the lipstick they'd purchased at Choi's and pinned her hair up to one side with the onyx barrette from Alexandre's, the look was complete. She came out wearing the form fitting dress, and instantly saw the effect it had on Leo.

His eyes narrowed and he slowly licked his lips in hungry appreciation. With a silent whirl of his finger, he directed her to turn around. As she did, he let out a long, low whistle. "I love your hair like that."

"Thank you." She came back around to face him and met his intense gaze. Waiting for him to say more, she heard her own breathing as if it was thunder. Why did his approval suddenly matter so much?

Leo gestured to the clerk. "What shoes do you have to go with this?"

Chagrinned, Zara looked down at her black three inch heels.

"I have just the thing." The sales clerk left them a second and returned with a pair of four inch red strappy sandals.

Standing four inch taller, Zara looked once again to Leo.

"Much better. So sexy. So provocative, and yet so expensive looking."

The hunger in his eyes made Zara shift and fidget. It was a powerful gaze that probed her, delved deep within her and brought out something wild and feral. A profusion of blood rushed to her cheeks, while a strong blast of sexual arousal set her thighs afire.

Leo stood and took a few quiet steps towards her, his eyes never losing their intensity. Zara didn't know what to think of him, of his sudden ardor. Was he simply toying with her? Her breath caught in her throat when he reached for her hand and the heat of her body shot up.

"Red suits you, my little vixen... so much more attractive than detective blue, don't you think?"

She wanted to smile, but couldn't. Her lips remained pouted in hunger, in anticipation of something more, something delicious and wonderful.

"Your red lips, your smoldering eyes, those sexy heels. I may never be able to look at you as a simple unassuming detective. All I'll see are the sensual lines of your breasts, the heavenly sweep of your waist and..." He bit his lower lip as he leaned over to glance at her rear end. "... a beautiful round ass I want to fill my hands with."

"Well, I do hope your lady friend appreciates it all."

"Lady friend?"

"Yeah, the girl you said you were buying all this for."

"Oh, I'm sure she'll love it. In fact, I'm sure she'll look hot in them, and I'm pretty sure I'm going to look forward to ripping off every stitch."

"How can you be so sure?"

He closed in and slipped his hands around her waist, letting them rest on the small of her back. "Because, my dear detective, every one of these designer garments is for you."

Tears of disbelief immediately sprung to her eyes. "Me?"

"I told you... I want the woman at my side to look hot, not like a school marm."

"So why the ruse? Why didn't you just come out and tell me?"

He shrugged. "I wanted to see your face when I mentioned another woman, and I wanted to see your face when you learned it was actually all for you. I have to say, I'm pleased with both; the touch of envy for that fictional woman, and the elation when you realized you were that woman. I was right about our first meeting. You want me as much as I want you."

"I what?" Zara asked, blushing.

"And now," Leo said ignoring her feeble denial, as he gestured to the clerk. "One final dress." He reached for the beautiful white linen dress with intricately embroidered hem and neckline. "Something a little casual for a day on the town. I thought we could have lunch somewhere."

Feeling a sudden pang of hunger, Zara took the dress and headed to the fitting room, only to find Leo following close behind her, a wide brimmed hat and delicate sandals in hand. He set the items on the seat inside the fitting room and looked expectantly at her.

"Need a hand getting out of that?"

"I don't think so," she said, waiting for him to leave.

"I think you do," he whispered as he turned her back to him. His heated fingers brushed along the nape of her neck and down her back as he drew the zipper down.

Conscious of her exposed skin, Zara stood straight and stiff, her breath caught in her lungs.

"Relax." Leo brought his hands to her shoulders and gently melted the tension away. "You've got to learn to relax." His voice was a hushed rasp in her ear.

UNASSUMED

Closing her eyes, Zara let her breath ease out of her lungs and the tension slip out of her fingertips. His touch was heaven and she wanted to discover the effects of an even more intimate touch.

Her wish was quickly granted when Leo pressed his lips to the nape of her neck. An aroused gasp escaped her and Leo responded by gently sucking on her flesh.

"Oh, my God, Leo. What are you doing?"

"Succumbing. Watching you these past hours has been very enlightening," he murmured. "It gives me a chance to look at you, to enjoy seeing your beauty, instead of the one being watched. I love how classic lines fit your body, and how clingy garments accentuate every curve. Most of all, I love the fiery look in your eyes when you see just how sexy you really are. Your innocence is so fresh yet sexy at the same time. And you're this amazing killing machine. You are the most fascinating woman I've ever met."

Zara backed into him, surprised by the hard strength of his chest as she let go and leaned into him.

"You're hot and you're sexy and you're gorgeous, but what really gets me, is that you don't know it."

She spun around to face him. "I've never had the luxury of wasting time on how I look. A quick ponytail and a comfortable uniform and I'm off."

"Yeah, I've kind of noticed that these past days. Even today; plain blue jeans and a ho hum shirt. It's a cool look, if you're planning on running down a criminal, but it won't cut it in my world."

Unhappy with his assessment of her, she pouted.

"Don't be offended. Despite your lack of fashion sense, you still look hotter than most women I know." His tongue snaked out to slowly run along his lips. "And your lips. How do you...?" He leaned in to touch his lips to hers "... taste." His mouth covered hers and took possession while his fingers clawed at her bare back. "Delicious."

Zara welcomed his tongue and eagerly took him in. He tasted fresh and masculine, and when she shyly brought her fingertips to his shoulders, she was mesmerized by the power and strength there.

"I want you," he whispered. "I want you so badly."

Her lips hungered for his, but she couldn't. She couldn't take a hold of them. Instead, she remained still, and desperately tried to ignore the carnival of thrilling sensations that was taking over her body.

"I can't," she finally whispered.

"Can't what?"

"This. I can't do this. I can't let myself get personally involved with you. I can't get this close to you."

"Your body seems pretty happy with the arrangement." His smile was playful, smoldering and filled with promise.

"Leo…"

"What is it? Are you afraid you'll lose control? Are you afraid to get close to someone because you don't want to risk losing them?"

"I'm not here for fun and games, Leo. I'm here to protect you. I'm here to do anything and everything to keep you out of harm's way, even take a bullet for you."

Shocked, he took a step back. "Take a bullet? I didn't know…"

"It's part of the job." She pulled away from him. "I can't lose sight of the job I'm here to do. Now, please let me get changed so we can get out of here."

His jaw tight, and his eyes hard with disappointment, he opened the door and left her.

Though her heart continued to beat with arousal, she quickly changed and resumed the look she was the most comfortable in; jeans and simple shirt.

Chapter 6

Leo

Leo sat in his office with thoughts of Zara blotting out all the important files that sat on his desk. First thing that morning, he'd sent her a thoughtful and understanding text telling her he accepted her decision and wouldn't hold it against her.. He would ignore his body's urge to seduce her and simply be content to work at her side.

At eight o'clock sharp, he called her office. "Can I see you in my office a moment?" Not waiting for a response, he hung up and waited. His body had a swift and strong reaction to the mere thought of seeing her again. She had an odd and unexpected effect on him, and while it troubled him, he relished the sense of excitement that took a hold of him. As he waited, he felt nervous and edgy. No woman had ever touched him so profoundly.

The door to his office opened and he stood to greet her, but instead of coming face to face with Zara in one of her newly purchased outfits, he was met by a handsome young man with wavy copper hair and light-colored eyes wearing a stylishly tailored suit.

Frowning, Leo shot a displeased look at the man. "Who the hell are you?"

"The name is Peter, sir," he said with a thick British accent as he scanned the spacious office. "Peter Brock."

"Where's Zara ?"

"She had a family emergency, sir. I know she's been doing a great job here, and believe me, sir, I intend to work just as hard." He peered beyond Leo's shoulder at the view of the harbor. "Exceptional view, sir. Very impressive."

Seething, Leo sat down and glared at the stranger. Since first waking up, he'd thought of the passionate kissed he'd shared with Zara and had been looking forward to seeing her again. He knew damn well the family emergency story was bullshit. She simply didn't have the guts to come in and face him that morning, and it pissed him off.

"Will she be in tomorrow?" Leo grumbled.

"I don't believe so, sir. Her grandmother has taken ill and Zara wanted to spend time with her."

"You can drop the 'sir' bit."

"My apologies. It's the London boy in me."

"Yeah, whatever." Glaring at the young Brit, he had a sense there was more to the story than he let on. "Tell me, why should I trust you? Who's to say you're who you say you are. For all I know you're some whack job who just walked in off the street."

"I assure you, sir… um, Mr. Lee, that I'm highly trained for this position." Peter pulled out a badge and flashed it at Leo. "I received my training in London and have been in Hong Kong for the past three years." Pride gleamed in his eyes as he put the badge away. "Zara and I have been working hard to capture the leaders and players in this crime ring for over a year. I know the dossier very well."

Leo took a closer look at Zara's replacement. He was a good looking guy, well over six feet tall, with a good build, chiseled jaw and piercing grey eyes. He seemed to be closing in on thirty, but he wore it well.

"How well do you know Zara," Leo asked on a hunch.

He peeled his eyes away from the door that led to Leo's private quarters. "Very well." The cocky arch of his brow told the story. He and Zara were close, or had once been. Zara was someone special to him.

"What are you looking for?" Leo said when he noticed Peter's searching gaze.

"I'm just taking it all in. The more familiar I am with my surroundings, the better equipped I am to do a good job. "Do you often have the opportunity to take a shower here?"

"It happens. I work long hours and going back home isn't always possible. Since I travel extensively, I can leave the office and head straight to the airport at a moment's notice. Just hop in the shower, change into a fresh suit and I'm off. Same goes for when I return from a business trip. I can come straight here without stopping at home first."

"How convenient." He seemed far from impressed by the explanation. "Has Zara had a need for a shower yet?"

"That's a peculiar question." He knew Peter was fishing for something and he decided to goad him on. "But yes. In a rush to a business meeting, I recently needed her assistance. She helped me get dressed."

"What an odd function for an assistant," Peter said with ill-concealed displeasure. "And who would think a grown man would need help getting dressed? Is this a part of the job I should look forward to?"

"Hardly," Leo said. "I'd happen to celebrate the opening of my new restaurant a little too heavily. I was somewhat hung over the next morning and Zara helped keep me stay steady."

"Oh. How fortunate for you."

No need to get snide, Leo wanted to say, but truth was, he enjoyed toying with the man who obviously held some affection for Zara. For a long moment they stared at one another, squaring off and sizing up.

"Is there any way I could reach Zara?" Leo finally said. "She'd started looking at the personal profiles of my employees and I'd like to know if she's learned anything interesting."

"I was perusing those very files when you called me to your office, sir. So far everything looks fine."

"Still, I would like to talk to Zara personally. Would you happen to know where she is exactly?"

"I believe she took her grandmother to the hospital. Which one, I couldn't tell you."

Leo still didn't believe him, and he fully intended to call Zara on her cell phone once Peter left the office. "That will be all for today, Peter. You can take the rest of the day off." He had no intention of spending the day with that man following him around.

"I'm afraid I can't do that. Zara left strict orders. I am not to let you out of my sight. The order of the day, sir; where you go, I go. The furthest I'll be from you is in my office."

"Fine," Leo muttered. "But leave me a little breathing space, will you?" His curt nod was Peter's cue to leave the office.

The moment the door closed, Leo dialed Zara's number, but when he got her voicemail, he hung up. Something told him she wouldn't call back if he left a message. He'd have to try to reach her some other way.

Prepared to placate Peter, he passed by his office on the way to the boardroom. "I'll be in a meeting with the board members for the next two hours if you need me."

"Perfect, sir."

After the board meeting, Leo once again popped his head in Peter's office. I'll be with developers in my office for the next hour.

"Perfect, sir."

With the meeting over, he visited Peter once more. "I'll have lunch in my office."

"Ditto here, sir."

Leo closed the door and rolled his eyes up to the ceiling. "Ditto here, sir," he muttered, mimicking Peter.

He had a quiet lunch alone in his office, but felt trapped and in a desperate need to get away. Seeing how Peter had settled in so comfortably, he decided to pay him one last visit.

"I'm having a meeting with the staff. Do you want to participate?"

Peter held up an employee file. "Too much work here. I'll pop in on the next one."

"Perfect," Leo said, and as he closed the door behind him, he smiled.

With purposeful steps, he headed to the elevators and took the first one down to the parking garage. Behind the wheel of his silver Mercedes, he took off. "Free at last," he said as he directed the car to the hospital. If nothing else, he wanted to know if this was all a lie.

And if it was true, he wanted to show Zara that he was there for her.

Chapter 7

Leo

Assuming Zara's grandmother still lived in Kowloon, Leo asked his GPS to find the clinics and hospitals in the neighborhood and headed to the first one on the list; Victoria's Health Clinic. He distinctly remembered Peter mentioning the name Victoria over the course of the morning and felt sure it was the right one.

It'd been a while since he'd driven himself around. Accustomed to having a hired chauffeur at his disposal at all times, the only times he ever got behind the wheel of a car was when he wanted the thrill of a speedy ride. However, driving around town had never been his idea of fun, and as he rounded the corner and approached the rundown hospital, he remembered why he hated driving in the city. The narrow streets were congested and finding a parking spot was virtually impossible.

UNASSUMED

Though he disliked the idea of appearing like a careless and spoiled billionaire, he parked his sporty car in a no parking zone. Paying a fine was of little importance, all things considered.

He shook his head and chuckled as he got out of the car. Who would have ever thought the heir to billions would forego the chauffeured limo and drive himself to such a neighborhood? It was hard to believe this was what his life had become; always on guard, always on the lookout and always with Zara giving him pointers on how to stay safe, like insisting he send his chauffeur away on paid leave. The same had been suggested for the greater part of his household staff.

"You can never be too cautious," she'd said. "Sometimes your enemies can lurk right under your nose."

After a thorough profile check, she'd reluctantly agreed to let him have one housekeeper come in to clean up once a week, but she'd insisted she be there whenever the small, older woman came in.

"That's their favorite method of getting close," she'd gone on to say. "They infiltrate the very household of their intended victim."

He smiled at her thoroughness, and marveled at how he'd come to enjoy his time with her within such a short amount of time. Barely two weeks after first meeting her, he found himself thinking of her almost constantly. He admired her bravery, and while having an undercover cop around him unnerved him at first, it was easy to put that aside and simply enjoy his time with her.

Until that morning when Peter showed up. Strange how only a few hours without her had him sneaking out of his office to find her.

He missed her… already. It made no sense, but it was there all the same.

He walked up to the front of the hospital and looked up and down the street then up at the shabby building with the graffiti covered door. This was the neighborhood Zara had grown up in, the type of neighborhood he'd heard about, read about, had seen on television, but had never, ever set foot in himself.

All of his life had been on the prosperous side of Hong Kong, and while he'd always been vaguely aware of the poverty so many people lived in, it had always been something distant and abstract. The type of thing stylish fundraisers with tiny finger sandwiches and French champagne were meant to aid.

Now, the reality of that poverty was right in his face. He looked up at the high rises around him. How many people lived high above in penthouse slums? How many people shared apartments smaller than his ensuite bathroom at home?

More than anything he wondered, how had Zara managed to come out of such a dreaded childhood so well balanced and smart. She'd must have had to grow a thick skin…that much was clear. She had the beauty of an aristocrat. She must have stood out like a bright flower or target in this neighborhood filled with seedy characters. He could easily imagine the men who'd harassed her, who'd attempted to get sexual favors in exchange for…

Disturbed by the notion, he shook his head, wanting to punch every man who dared treat her less than the lady she was. He wanted to take her out of this dark and dangerous world and keep her safe. He wanted to protect her, care for her. She may be tough, but he saw the sweet little vulnerable girl in her when she told him about her parents. He saw the real woman that was underneath the detective, and boy did he wanted her.

He coughed, partially to clear his throat of the stale air, but mostly to rid himself of the sense of despair that suddenly draped over him.

Almost hoping he wouldn't find Zara in such dismal surroundings, he took another look at the building. The place was so horribly rundown it was hard to imagine anyone coming out in better health than when they'd gone in.

Hiding his disdain, he entered the clinic. "Why didn't you call me, Zara?" he quietly said to himself. He could have easily made arrangements to have her grandmother admitted to the best hospital in Hong Kong. A quick phone call and she would have had the best care Hong Kong could provide.

The smell inside had him instantly gagging and he pulled his handkerchief out of his pocket and brought it over his mouth. The stench, part urine, part blood, and part death with a drop of disinfectant thrown in, was overwhelming.

He followed the narrow corridor and found a nurse's station, but no nurse in sight. After waiting a moment, a young woman arrived and hurried behind the counter.

"I'm looking for Zara Zee," Leo said as he shoved his handkerchief back into his pocket. "I believe she came in last night with her grandmother."

The young woman barely glanced at him as she picked up a few rags and a bucket from the corner. Before she could walk away, Leo took a hold of her forearm.

"Please, I'm looking for a young woman, Zara Zee, and..."

"Sorry," she said with a shrug. "I no can tell you."

Letting her go, he bit his lip and knew he'd have to explore the small hospital on his own. He turned down the first hallway and peered into the first room. After taking a careful look at the eight beds crowded into the small stuffy room, he moved on to the next room and the next and the next.

Finally in the third crowded room, he saw a young girl seated by a bed at the far end of the room. With her back to the door, she sat facing an elderly person in the small cot.

Leo quietly made his way to her, careful not to disrupt the other patients who moaned and groaned for their aches and pains.

"Zara," he whispered as he put his hand to her shoulder.

The young girl turned to him, her brow creased in question.

"I'm so sorry," he said as he realized he'd been mistaken.

Pulling in a deep breath, he quietly left the room. "Where are you, Zara?" he muttered to himself.

Retracing his steps, he returned to the nurse's station, saw no one, and continued into the hallway facing it. Soon he arrived at what appeared to be a feeble attempt at a cafeteria.

Dozens of people sat at two long plywood tables, their heads hung low over tepid cups of coffee or tea they'd purchased from one of the three vending machines set along the wall.

A quick glimpse around and he knew Zara wasn't there either. With no other options, he pulled out his phone to call her. Even if she didn't answer, he should be able to hear the phone ring from even the furthest corner of the small hospital.

UNASSUMED

From the far end of the cafeteria came the muffled sound of a cell phone ringing. Following the sound, he shimmied between the crowded chairs and came to the vending machine that sold chocolate bars and potato chips.

Though still muffled, the sound came from close by. Under the glare of many of the people seated at the long tables, he lifted the pale blue blazer atop the vending machine and saw the bling of Zara's phone. It was unmistakable; colorful gemstones, a snowflake and the Eiffel tower embellished her unique phone. He'd been surprised to see Zara pull out the flashy phone, the only instance in which she allowed herself an explosion of expression.

Picking it up, he stared at it as it continued to ring. If her phone was here, where was she?

He turned off his phone to stop the ringing. Filled with questions, he turned to the people at the table. "Where's the girl who left her phone here?"

Many of them shook their heads and many more shrugged before turning away. One old man raised a shaky hand and pointed down the hall.

With a pat on the old man's shoulder, Leo thanked him and hurried out of the cafeteria and down the hall. He passed an operating room and immediately came to a small waiting room. In the corner, tucked up on the old dusty sofa was a frail girl in faded jeans and a pink hoodie.

"Zara," Leo said as he came to her, his hand instantly going to her brow. "Zara."

She didn't move, or stir, or budge. Completely knocked out, she remained deep in sleep.

Realizing that she'd probably been up all night, he decided to let her sleep. At least he knew where she was and he'd be there for her the moment she awoke. Poor girl, she'd even forgotten her phone on the vending machine, she was so tired.

At the sound of footsteps, Leo turned to see a nurse heading into the operating room.

"Excuse me. Please." He hurried up to the nurse. "Who are they operating on?"

The woman simply stared at him.

Leo pointed to Zara. "Is it her grandmother? An older woman? Is she the one they're operating on?"

Tightlipped, but compassionate, the woman nodded.

"This woman is very important to me," Leo said, still pointing at Zara. "And her grandmother means everything to her. Please make sure the surgeon does his best to do whatever this woman needs."

The nurse nodded. "Surgery start early this morning," she said. "They should be almost finish."

"I plan on making a huge donation to this hospital. Tell them that. Tell them to be especially careful and diligent with this patient. Lots of money. Money for equipment. Money to repair and renovate."

Pursing her lips, she glared at him. "Doctors always do best, no matter who you are, no matter how much you pay. We do our best." With a huff, she turned on her heel and left him.

He'd obviously offended her and the establishment for which she worked, but he didn't have time to get caught up in remorse. Returning to Zara, he knelt down in front of her.

So innocent, so frail, she was far from the mighty and ferocious police officer who whipped up a fierce martial art move at the drop of a hat. His instinct told him to pull her into his arms, to hold her tight and promise to protect her forever, but when she stirred, he froze and readied himself for the tears and emotion that were sure to come.

114

But after a few unintelligible utterances, she curled up once more and slept soundly. In the silence of the small waiting room, the sudden strident sound of her phone ringing made Leo jump. He didn't want a phone call to awaken her so he hurried to pull the phone out, but when he saw the caller, he stared at the screen a moment: Peter Brock. What the hell did he want with Zara?

If he continued to let it ring, Zara would surely wake up, but if he answered, he'd have to talk to the man, and that was the last thing he wanted to do. Making a snap decision, he left the waiting room to return to the hall and switched the phone to text mode with the intention of answering Peter as if he were Zara .

Sorry, still at the hospital. Can't really talk right now.

I understand, Peter replied

What do you want?

Have you seen Lee?

Lee? No. Why? Did you lose him?

No.

Liar, Lee thought. You lost me over an hour ago.

UNASSUMED

He had a few meetings earlier this morning and must've stepped out for a minute. How's your grandmother?

In surgery. Getting back to Lee, I think I'll be able to watch over him starting tomorrow morning. I won't need you to step in.

About that... I've come to realize that assigning you to Lee wasn't a good idea to begin with.

Why would you say that? I've enjoyed working with him.

For starters, he's a bit of a womanizer. I'm not really comfortable having you around a guy like that.

Lee smiled. So he was getting under Peter's skin.

Why would you be uncomfortable with the job I have to do? Lee wrote, hoping to get more information from Peter.

Zara, you know how I feel about you. I don't want to leave you in a position where a man like Lee can take advantage of you. Plus, I'm your superior and you're my responsibility. I have to ensure you're capable of performing your job, and I'm not so sure you can around Lee.

I'm in a perfect position to watch and protect Lee. We know from past kidnappings that they get in close to their victims before taking action. I need to stay close to him, and being his assistant allows me that proximity. Believe me, I'm so unassuming, no one would ever guess I was a cop.

I know you're a talented and professional detective, Zara, but I just want to take care of you. A man like Lee can't help but want to get into your pants. As unassuming as you might think you are, you're always ravishing and no man can resist you. You know the hard time I've had resisting you. Believe me, I've tried to think of you purely as a detective, but I can't.

So Peter really did have a thing for Zara. He'd suspected it right from the start, but seeing it written out came as a blow all the same. Frowning, Leo read the text three times before finally answering.

You're my superior, Peter, and you can't allow yourself to think of me that way. In fact, your unprofessional behavior is even worse than Lee trying to get together with me. Do you have any idea how uncomfortable all this makes me feel? If you did than you would stop.

117

UNASSUMED

I apologize. Did I really read you so wrong? We had a few enjoyable dates, and I thought you had a good time with me. And when you came to London for the holidays. We had a smashing time together... didn't we? And the time you spent at my country estate. My parents loved you, they found you interesting and entertaining and they've been looking forward to seeing you again. Are you saying all that meant nothing to you?

Leo didn't answer. An intense and unfamiliar sense of jealousy took over him as he thought of Zara with the Brit. She'd visited Peter's home. She'd met his family. Yet, as he prepared to answer Peter, he felt a bit of sympathy for the man who obviously had big plans for his relationship with Zara.

Look, if that's how you really feel about it, about me, I can ask for a transfer, Peter wrote.

That might be a good idea.

You mean a lot to me, Zara., certainly more than this job. I'll ask for a transfer first thing tomorrow morning, if that's what you really want.

Leo almost heard Peter's heart breaking in the text, and once again, a sense of sympathy and guilt took hold. Having known Zara for only two weeks and feeling such an intense desire to be with her, to protect and possess her, he could easily understand how Peter had fallen so hard and fast for her.

Closing his eyes, he questioned what he'd just done. He had no right to play with her life like that. He opened his eyes and looked at Zara's phone in his hand.

He already had so much on his plate; inheriting his father's estate, heading Lee Holdings, and meeting with Errol to discuss the Oyster House.

He looked at the screen and finally sent a message;

Don't worry about me and Lee, and I don't want you to transfer. Just give me a bit of time and some space. I don't want to feel rushed into anything. Besides, Lee's case is just getting interesting and I wouldn't want to miss out on that.

All right. Take your time and be with your grandmother as long as you need. I'll see you tonight.

Tonight? Leo thought. They were hooking up that night?

No, Leo texted back. *I'm supposed to be going to Lee's restaurant tonight.*

UNASSUMED

I thought you were taking the night off, and with all the stress you must be going through with your grandmother, I wanted to do something special for you. I have to admit, I'm looking forward to seeing your beautiful face. I don't mean to put the pressure on, but I do love you, Zara. Very much.

Leo's face heated up and his gut tied in a knot.

Got to go, he texted plainly.

He ended the conversation and quickly deleted the thread. Feeling a little foolish, he returned to the waiting room. "Zara," he said softly, but the room was empty. "Great. Now where'd she go?"

More importantly, how had she not seen him just outside the waiting room?

He took to the hall and continued down to the next intersection. Looking to the right, all he could see were piles of damp boxes leaning up against the wall. Looking to the left, his heart stopped.

Two men held onto either side of Zara as they tried to shove her into the rusted old freight elevator. Still drowsy, her feeble attempts to get away had no effect on the burly men who dragged her inside.

Leo wasted no time running up to the trio. Just as the elevator door was about to close, he thrust his foot in the gap, preventing it from shutting further.

"What the…?" one of the men cried out.

Leo pushed the door open, grabbed Zara's wrist and yanked her out of the elevator, letting the doors close behind her. With the men's expletives echoing through the door, he pulled Zara down the hall.

"Come on! Quick!" he shouted as he ran down the hall.

"Leo? What's going on? My grandmother. I…" Confused, she followed behind him.

"My car's just down the street. Hurry, Zara."

"What are you doing here? Isn't Peter watching over you?"

"I gave him the slip." Seeing the shock on her face, he added, "When you didn't show up at the office… I had to come find you."

"Did he tell you my grandmother was in the hospital?"

He nodded. "I didn't believe him. I thought you were just trying to avoid me. I had to come see for myself. Besides…" He turned to quickly look at her.

"If it was true, I wanted to be here for you. You shouldn't have to go through this alone."

Just when he thought they should come upon the front door, Leo realized he'd made a wrong turn somewhere. This way," he said taking another corridor. They arrived at the front doors in time to see the two burly men running out of the hospital. "Shit." He yanked Zara back and for a moment they pressed back against the wall.

Zara looked up at him, her eyes wide with fright, but before she could open her mouth to question him, Leo brought his finger over his pursed lips and mouthed, "Quiet."

"Bitch," one of the men grunted as they came back inside. "I thought you said they went this way."

"I did. I could've sworn... There's no other way in or out. Shit the guy is fast."

"Did you really think Leopold Lee was just a pretty boy who brought it to the movie screen? The bastard's the real deal. The guy's in shape and he can run like nobody's business."

"Fuck him. I just want to get the girl back. What the hell do you want to do now? Head out to her grandmother's place and wait for her there?"

"I don't care what we have to do to get her back. I want that girl. She's the guy's fucking assistant. She has access to what we need and I know we can crack into the network with her help. I'm not about to let her slip through our fingers."

Leo's heart pounded in his ears as he listened to the men talk about them.

"Her grandmother."

"Come again?"

"Her grandmother is still here. Zara'll have no choice but to come back to see her sometime. If we stay close to the old lady, we're sure to get our hands on her."

The silence thickened, and Zara looked up at Leo with concern clearly marring her brow.

"Yeah," the goon said. "And when she does come back, we'll get her to work for us."

Frowning with anger, Zara pushed off the wall, but Leo quickly pulled her back.

"Now is not the time," he said in a quiet hush.

"Did you hear what they said?" she hissed. "That's my grandmother they're talking about."

He nodded his understanding of her frustration, but still held on tight.

123

"Let's go see if the old lady's out of surgery."

Her face red and her eyes turning something akin to maniacal, Zara struggled against Leo's hold. Only when they no longer heard the men's footsteps did Leo finally release her.

"Those idiots are going after my grandmother at her most vulnerable, and you want to stop me from going after them?" Turning on her heel, she headed after them.

"Be sensible, Zara." Gripping her wrist, he pulled her back to him. "You're letting your emotions get the better of you."

"No. You're being a careless macho man who doesn't know what it's like to care so much about someone. Now, let go of me."

Leo winced at her words, and considered letting her go, but couldn't. "Your grandmother is still in surgery. They can't get to her. Besides, you heard them. It's you they really want. They want to use her to get to you, and we can't let that happen. How much help are you going to be to your grandmother if these men get a hold of you." Pensive and concerned, he thought a moment before going on. "We have to be smart... smarter than them. We know they want you and with that knowledge, we can make our own game plan."

     Looking at him, she smiled.

     "What are you up to now?" he said.

     "You'll see."

Chapter 8

Zara

Zara still couldn't believe that Leopold Lee had come to the hospital to find her, but she hid her giddiness behind a professional façade. She was thrilled he'd missed her and she'd almost let slip how much she'd been thinking of him since running out on their shopping spree.

Since arriving at the hospital late the night before, she'd had plenty of time to sit and wait and think, and more often than not, it was Leo who crawled into her thoughts. He'd been so kind and generous, and she'd repaid him by turning her back on him.

Looking at him, so stylishly handsome with his hair swept back, his tight muscles well concealed in a perfect tan suit and his butt... No matter what pants he wore, she had trouble tearing her eyes off his exquisite backside. He really had it all – looks, charm, charisma, and a darn sexy butt. No wonder he was very popular amongst women, although an action star, and men.

"What do you have in mind, my dear detective?" Leo said as he looked tenderly at her.

"Playing into their hands."

He cocked his head to the side in the most engaging manner and Zara just wanted to run her hand along his cheek and push her fingers into his hair. She wanted to lose herself in him and completely erase the past twenty-four hours.

"I'm going to just go out there and innocently walk right into their trap."

Taking a step closer to her, he grinned. "You are devilishly wicked, and I love it, in theory, but this isn't a movie, Zara. So many things can go wrong."

Her body wanted to explode as thrill after thrill rushed through her. His smile was divine, and damn it if he didn't look so freaking hot. It was all she could do to keep from pressing up to his hard, muscular chest. "I have to find out what they want from me," she said with professionalism. "And if I'm right in there with them, while you know exactly where I am, it'll be a piece of cake."

"Yeah, don't bet on that."

"Don't underestimate me. They want me to work with them in order to get what they want from you. I'll just play along." Beaming, she looked up at him. "I'm really good at playing along."

"So I've noticed."

"I've been waiting for this chance since first learning about this crime ring. I'm not about to let this chance pass me by."

"Okay. I'm on board, but reluctantly so. It's too dangerous, Zara."

"It's the break I've been waiting for to infiltrate, Leo. It'll be worth it if I can crack this crime ring and get to the bottom of it all..."

Leo sighed. "What do you want me to do?"

"Nothing. Just hang back."

He seemed uncertain.

"And don't worry about being protected. Peter's great at what he does and he'll look out for you while I'm in with these guys. Just relax and trust him."

Leo grimaced. "I'd much rather have you looking out for me."

"No," she corrected. "You'd rather have me at your beck and call. You'd rather have me following you around, dressing up the way you want and being the pretty little thing on your arm."

"Seriously, Zara."

"Seriously, Leo. I have to do this. Go back to your office, talk to Peter and tell him where I am. Everything will be fine." She turned away.

"Zara," Leo called.

She turned back to him. "What?"

"They saw you running away with me. Won't that make them suspicious?"

Taking in his words, she stopped a moment.

"I know you really want to bust this ring, but it all seems so risky and dangerous." He walked right up to her and slipped his hands around her waist pulling her closer.

She instantly remembered the hot and steamy kiss they'd shared and longed to share another. Her heart beat with tons of adrenaline and the thrill of the hunt as she considered infiltrating the crime ring, but it also beat for him; this man who was at once strong and sexy, yet so sensitive and caring.

"I know what I'm doing, Leo. I promise. Everything will run smoothly. That's my grandmother in that operating room. It's only natural that I come back to check up on her. They won't suspect a thing because I won't do anything to compromise my chance of becoming one of them."

UNASSUMED

"I don't want anything to happen to you," he said as he pulled her closer.

"I don't want anything to happen to me, either." Though she tried to laugh off his concern, her heart was thrilled by it. She shivered beneath his intense touch and knew it would be so easy to succumb to him.

"I couldn't live with myself if you got hurt because of me," he whispered.

"This is my job, Leo. Whether it's to save you, or any other citizen, this is what I have to do." Though she tried to sound flippant, she was struck by the emotions in his eyes.

He pulled in closer, his lips just inches from hers. She could smell him, the sweet scent of his expensive cologne over the strong masculine scent of the man he was.

"Leo," she said in a husky voice that didn't belong to her. Breathing became difficult, talking was impossible and thinking clearly was out of the question. All that mattered in that moment were his lips so close to hers. All the mattered were his hands over her body, and her hands that longed to return the favor. All that mattered was him, right there, so close to her. "I'm trying to do my job as best as…"

He cupped her face and gently brought his lips over hers.

Her body's response was electric and she let out an enraptured sigh as the small, gentle kiss became a passionate and all-consuming embrace. His soft lips coddled hers while his tongue explored her mouth, drawing gasp after gasp of pleasure and desire.

All the tension of the past day and night melted away as she pressed into him, reveling in his strength and eager to discover more. She let go of her concern for her ailing grandmother, set aside her confused feelings for Peter and simply concentrated on Leo and his mouth, and his tongue, and his lips.

"Oh, Leo," she moaned as she tried to regain some sort of composure. "I have to… This isn't the time for… Oh, I just can't. Not now. Not here."

"And yet I want to do so much more than just kiss you. I want to devour you, to taste every inch of you. I want to run my tongue up your thigh and really make you groan with pleasure."

Shocked, she looked up at him. "Leo!"

"Don't play innocent. Your kiss was the fiery and passionate kiss of a woman in need, not the shy embrace of a young girl who *can't*."

"Still…"

"All I want to do is take you away from this stinky hospital and carry you into a luxurious hotel room. I want to lay with you, sleep with you, hold you in my arms until the sun comes up." A devilish grin curved his lips. "I want to feel your body pressed up against mine…naked and glowing with after-sex sweat."

"Leo." She took a step back, horrified not so much by his words, but by her body's reaction to them. Her thighs clenched and she felt a definite patch of moisture in her panties. "I can't be thinking of all this right now."

"Then just tell me you want me."

"What?"

"Just tell me you want me, Zara."

"Leo. I don't have time to play games."

"Say it."

Licking her lips, she tried to muster up the nerve to lie to him, but she knew her body had already betrayed her. "Yes, but not like this. My grandmother is probably out of surgery by now and she'll be waking up soon. I want to be there when she wakes up."

"You won't be able to if those goons snatch you up."

"I'll just have to hope they'll be reasonable and let me see her before they cart me away."

"All right, but I'm coming with you."

"No."

"Yes."

"Leo, this is serious police business, not some action movie set. You said so yourself; things don't always go as planned. The bullets that come out of their guns are real. The blood that spills at the hands of these men is real. And when someone falls to the ground dead, they don't get back up when the director yells 'cut'. So please, stay out of it and let me do my job."

For a moment he looked hurt, then angry, then offended. Zara wanted to laugh by the array of emotions her comment garnered. "No offense," she said.

"I'm not just a lowly actor who pretends to know a few karate moves. I can defend myself and I can protect you, as a man who cares for a woman should."

Zara didn't know what to say. Flattered by his words, she knew she still had to look at the situation with a professional eye.

"I know you're tough, Zara, and you're well trained, but I saw you when those men dragged you to the elevator. I also felt the fear. The fear of what could happen to you if they walked out of here with you." He brushed the back of his fingers along her cheek. "Don't you see? I've finally found a woman I care about, and you're asking me to let her walk into danger... and for what? So she can protect me? No, I'm the one who should be protecting you."

He pulled her in for a long, hard kiss filled with love and tenderness. "I want to protect you. I want to keep you safe." He looked intently into her eyes. "Don't you get it? I want you, Zara."

"That doesn't make sense. We just met a few..."

"I've spent more time with you these past weeks than with anyone else... ever. But it's not the amount of time we've spent together that really matters, it's how I've felt every single time. You make me forget that I'm an action movie star. With you I'm not the heir to Lee Holdings. I'm just a man, relaxed, and happy, and normal. I'm myself, the good and not so good real self. You've been around me when I'm angry, and impatient..." He smiled remembering the first time she walked into his office. "And even hung over."

And almost completely naked, Zara wanted to add.

"I'm flattered you feel so comfortable around me, but that still doesn't..."

She heard the familiar ring tone of her phone and cast a curious glance at Leo's breast pocket, the source of the sound.

Rather sheepishly, he pulled it out and handed it to her. "I found it in the cafeteria when I was looking for you. You must've been really concerned about your grandmother to leave it behind like that."

She nodded and took the phone. "It's the hospital," she said as she looked at the screen. "Hello, yes. Yes, I'm at the hospital at this very moment. I'll be right there." Looking up at Leo, she slipped the phone into her pocket. "She's out of surgery, and should be waking up any minute now, but the doctor wants to talk to me."

"Perfect. I'll be right behind you."

"Okay." She no longer had time to argue the point. "But keep a reasonable distance."

"As far away as I can while still keeping an eye on you."

"If it makes you feel better, but just so you know, I won the Iron Fist Martial Arts Championship two years in a row a few years back. I may be petite, but I can pack a punch. Believe it or not, I can throw down a man three times my size. I've learned to take pretty good care of myself, Mr. Action Movie Star."

"I don't doubt that you're a dynamo, but I'll still be close by." Leo kissed her forehead then urged her forward.

Eager to learn about her grandmother's status, she headed to the room the doctor had asked her to meet him in; down the hall, first door around the corner.

After knocking lightly, she opened the door expecting to see her grandmother lying in bed with the doctor at her side, but the sole bed in the darkened room was empty and there was no one in the room.

"Grandma?" she called. Seeing a narrow door by the far wall, she walked to it and opened it, expecting to see a small bathroom, but it was a dark linen closet filled with stacks of rolled up sheets.

Confused, she took a step back, but before she could turn around a black hood fell over her head, instantly blinding her. She tried to scream, but a thick hand pressed over her mouth as another hand pushed her head up against the wall.

Her hands were roughly yanked behind her back and handcuffs were squeezed tight over each wrist. Fighting to free herself, Zara kicked as best she could, but with every jagged breath she inhaled of the strange herbal scent that filled the cloth hood, she felt sleepier and sleepier.

Chapter 9

Leo

Leo watched Zara round the corner then hurried to take a peek into the corridor she'd taken. In the distance, he saw her stop before a door, tap gently on it and entered.

He waited a moment or two before taking to the corridor, whistling a light tune as he nonchalantly made his way to the door. Putting on the charm, he smiled at a passing nurse, and nodded politely at an old man who seemed in a rush to find a bathroom, something for which the hospital seemed to be sorely lacking.

Still whistling, he arrived at the door Zara had disappeared behind. For a quiet moment he listened at the door, expecting to hear the doctor give Zara an update on her grandmother's status, but there was only silence, hard, cold silence.

A chill ran up the back of his neck and he knew something was wrong. Not bothering to knock, he opened the door to find it completely empty save for a small, vacant bed.

"Zara," he called out though he didn't truly expect a response. He opened the door to a closet filled with bed linens, then opened the door beside it. It opened onto an adjacent room, something akin to an office, with filing cabinets and a few small tables, but no desk. "Zara."

It couldn't be. She couldn't have disappeared so fast. He was right there. If anyone had emerged into the corridor, from any room, he would have seen them. He returned to the hall and investigated a few more rooms, but only found bedridden patients.

Maybe he'd been mistaken from the start. The corridor was long... maybe she'd taken another door, maybe...

He approached the nurse's station.

"Please, I'm looking for Zara Zee. Her grandmother just came out of surgery."

The nurse smiled, more star struck than helpful. "Zara who?"

"Zara Zee."

The nurse looked down at her list of patients. "The only patient to recently come out of surgery is in room eleven." She pointed down the hall. "It's right down there."

"Thank you." He rushed off, counting down the rooms as he went. Twenty-one, nineteen, fourteen. Eleven. He stopped and took a deep breath. She'd better be in there.

He quietly opened the door. A small old woman slept soundly in the middle of the bed, but no Zara. Taking a step closer to the woman, he wondered if it was really Zara's grandmother. Perhaps the nurse was mistaken, but no. There was no mistake. The woman was old, but her skin was tight along her cheekbones, cheekbones as high and aristocratic as Zara's, and her lips still retained their youthful pucker, so similar to the lips he'd just kissed.

It was as if he were looking into Zara's future. "Not bad," he said as he had an instant glimpse of his life with Zara, growing old with her. "But where the hell are you?"

Lost and confused, he returned to the first room and examined it more closely. Then he saw it; a window by the far corner. It opened onto the vacant lot beside the hospital. It was wide open and just outside, below the window sill, were two sets of extra large footsteps clearly stamped into the damp mud.

Taking a step back, he slipped on something and almost fell back. On the floor at his feet was a small chocolate pearl, just like the ones that had dangled from the earrings he'd bought her on their shopping spree. His heart pounded at the thought of the struggle that had ripped the precious pearl from her ear. But then he noticed where the struggle had ceased.

A flurry of short scuff marks marred the floor around the pearl, but two long black streaks led from the fallen pearl to the open window. "What'd they do to you, baby?"

Feeling panicked and guilty, he pulled out his phone and called his office.

"Lee Holdings. How may I…"

"It's Lee," Leo cut in. "Is Peter Brock around?"

"He's standing right in front of me."

"Put him on."

"Hello," the British voice said.

"Peter, it's Lee."

"Well, well, well. Mr. Lee. You're a clever gent, aren't you?"

"No time for games, Brock. Zara just went missing."

"She what?"

"I was right behind her as she went in to see her grandmother, but when I walked into the room not long after, she was gone. Nothing in the room. Nobody."

"You're at the hospital?"

"Yes," he said with irritation.

"You escaped my watchful eye so you could go out looking for Zara? I should've known. I thought I'd noticed something odd in your eyes when I mentioned her name."

"Did you hear me? She's gone."

"Maybe she just gave you the slip. Zara can be very hard headed when she chooses to be."

"Listen closely. I found her sleeping in the waiting room. I stepped out for a minute and when I returned two burly men were carting her off. I managed to snatch her back, but we overheard them talking. They had a plan to get her, to get her to work for them. She knowingly walked into their trap thinking she could outsmart them, but it looks like they're having the last laugh."

"Zara's highly trained. No one could simply..."

"But they did. Are you going to just stay there and argue the point or are you going to do something about it?"

"Don't move. I'll be right there. Stay put."

Leo hung up, but staying put was out of the question. He had to do something. He jumped out the window and tried to track the footsteps as long as he could, but the moment they hit the pavement, there was nothing else to follow. Slowly filling with desperation, he returned to the open window and crawled back in. "What happened in here?" He looked around the barren room, taking a close look at everything. There had to be something he hadn't noticed before.

Then his eye finally caught on a flash of white under the bed. He bent down to pick up a small slip of paper, hoping it held relevant information.

Da Hwa Factory.

Leo stared at the letterhead and frowned. The name was familiar, too familiar. He knew he'd heard it before, but couldn't remember where or in what context. Closing his eyes, he replayed news reports from television and articles he'd read in the paper, all while knowing the name should mean so much more than that.

Lee Holdings. Da Hwa had something to do with Lee Holdings. He quickly ran through some of the more recent meetings he'd attended and finally remembered when he'd heard the name. Da Hwa had been the main topic of one of those meetings, but why?

It suddenly came to him and he opened his eyes to stare at the letterhead. He owned Da Hwa Factory, but that didn't explain how the company's letterhead ended up in the very spot where Zara had disappeared?

Once again, he pulled out his phone. "Liu. Take out everything you have on Da Hwa Factory and put it on my desk."

"Sir? Everything?"

"Everything." He hung up and turned around to see Peter walking in.

Chapter 10

Leo

"You shouldn't have given me the slip like that," Peter said with a frown. He stood at the door with his feet firmly planted on the old linoleum floor.

"Sometimes a man's gotta do what he's gotta do."

"No. Sometimes billionaire playboys think they can do whatever the hell they choose to do. Just because you're the heir to Lee Holdings doesn't give you the right to play with Hong Kong's police department any way you please. This isn't all fun and games, you know. This isn't a movie set."

"I know."

"Then act like it. Zara and I are risking our lives to protect you. The least you can do is keep the risks at a minimum. Running off like you did puts us all in danger." Peter walked around and looked closely at the room before bending down to examine the scuff marks on the floor. "This is where they got her, isn't it?"

Leo nodded.

"Looks like she managed to put up some kind of fight."

"She didn't make it easy for them."

Peter reached for the wastebasket in the corner and inspected the contents. Seeing something interesting, he pulled a pair of disposable chopsticks from his breast pocket.

"Did you find your lunch in there?" Leo said with a sarcastic snort.

Poking the chopsticks in the basket, Peter pulled out a soaked rag. "These things come in pretty handy when it comes to manipulating evidence without altering it. Tampering with evidence can be a real problem in an investigation." He took a whiff of the rag.

"Chloroform?"

Peter nodded. "No wonder she didn't get to fight them off enough. These bastards didn't even have the guts to fight her fair and square. They just sedated her and dragged her out." He followed the long black marks that led to the window. "Bastards."

146

He turned to Leo. "Zara's in this predicament because of you, you know?"

Unhappy with the comment, Leo frowned, but kept his calm. "She's in this predicament because you assigned her to protect me. You knew the situation was dangerous and you still put her on this case."

"This is an important case, and any young detective would want to sink their teeth into it. Zara's ambitious, but she's also dedicated to her work. She very much wanted to be on this case."

"If you'd done your research, if you'd known me at all, you would know that I'm very capable of defending myself, that I don't need protection."

"I think we're in a better position to make that decision than you are. We know what these ruthless and vicious criminals can do."

Leo snorted and looked out the window. "Whatever. Are we just going to stand here arguing the point or are we going to do something about it?"

Letting out an exasperated sigh, Peter ran his hands through his hair and looked at Leo. "My car's just outside."

"So's mine." He hurried out the door with Peter right behind him.

"Your car is a little too conspicuous to be around the factory," Peter said as he kept stride with Leo.

Leo's breath caught in his throat a moment, but he quickly swallowed it as he stared straight ahead. He hadn't shown Peter the letter head he'd found, so how could he know about Da Hwa Factory? He bit down on the questions he wanted to throw at Peter and decided to simply wait and see. "My car will get us there faster... and in comfort."

"I have a police cruiser. It's fast enough."

"Not enough to outrun these goons if they decide to take chase."

"We'll take the cruiser," Peter said with finality.

"I spent thousands customizing my car so that every need is met. There's no way in hell I'm going to drive out to the factory in a police cruiser." Leo stopped in front of the room where Zara's grandmother still lay.

"At least they didn't go after her," Peter said as he looked at the older woman.

"Yet," Leo added. "They know she's here and they'll no doubt return."

A nurse came in to tend to a patient in the crowded room, but Peter pulled her aside with one hand while diving into his pant pocket with the other to pull out a handful of bills. "Please put that woman in a private room," he said pointing to the frail sleeping woman.

The nurse stared at him and the bills with astonishment, but took the money and nodded.

"I'll be back later tonight to make sure she's been set up in a suitable room," he added for good measure.

Leo and Peter exited the stuffy and smelly room.

"That's pretty generous of you," Leo said.

"I know the old woman is tough, despite how fragile she looks in that bed, but a little pampering can't hurt."

"Not to mention making Zara happy."

Peter frowned as he pulled his phone out. "Chen, I'd like to have a guard…"

Leo turned his attention to the possible situation Zara found herself in while Peter finished his call. He'd managed to hide well just how worried he

149

was about her, but his gut was increasingly twisted into a painful knot.

"I'll sleep better knowing Zara's grandmother is well guarded," Peter said as he put his phone away.

"I'm sure Zara will appreciate that."

They pushed through the main entrance doors and stepped out on the filthy sidewalk. Without hesitating, Leo headed to his car and Peter begrudgingly followed. Leo beeped the doors open and took the driver's seat.

Once inside the car, Peter took a long moment to take in the elegant and sexy interior. "I see why you didn't want to take the cruiser."

"Not that I'm spoiled, but once you've had this degree of comfort and luxury, it's hard to fall back to the basics." He put the car in gear and took to the street. "Beside, I rarely get the chance to drive, and this will give me the chance to really take her out."

"Is this where I'm supposed to sympathize with the poor little rich boy?"

"Hey, don't hate me because I grew up with a few creature comforts."

"Let's be honest here, this is a little more than just creature comforts. You have a lifestyle that is beyond most people's wildest dreams."

"And I've worked hard for it, too. I've spent a lifetime acquiring the best things that life has to offer, and I make no qualms about that."

"Oh, please. Worked hard? You don't know what working hard is. Most people in Hong Kong, hell, all of China will work their fingers to the bone for their entire life and will never touch the kind of money you flippantly throw around during any given month."

Leo couldn't argue with that. Despite having worked hard all his life, he knew the greater part of his wealth hadn't come to him by way of work at all. It's simply been passed down to him by his hard working father.

"So going to the not so trendy part of Kowloon must've been quite the decent into hell," Peter added. "Have you ever seen anything like that hospital before?"

Leo's jaw tightened and the rancid smell of the hospital returned to aggravate his nostrils. "It's inhumane... that hospital. I could have set up Zara's grandmother in a comfortable and modern hospital."

"It's not so easy seeing how the other half lives, is it?" Peter tapped his fingers loudly on the armrest as he clucked his tongue in aggravation. "The other half lives... ha. It's more like the other ninety-nine percent."

Leo didn't want to get into a discussion about the haves and have nots. "And yet the men and women at that hospital are doing everything they can to help every patient. It's admirable." Admirable, yes, but he knew deep in his heart that he would have to do something to help them further. A few hundred thousand dollars could go a long way to make patients more comfortable and it would barely make a dent in his bank account.

"You and Zara are from such different worlds. For all the wealth and riches and luxuries that you have, you know nothing about what she finds truly precious."

"And you do?"

Peter nodded.

"Isn't there something in the police handbook about fraternizing...?"

After a light hearted chuckle, Peter looked at Leo. "Nobody knows this, but... Oh hell, I might as well tell you. We're practically engaged."

"You and Zara?" Leo said with disdain.

"Yep, and once we're married, she'll never have to worry about her grandmother again. Come to think of it, she'll never have to worry about anything again."

Seething, Leo gripped the wheel. "Where to?"

"Head north towards Guang Zhou."

Leo veered the sportscar onto the onramp and they were soon on the highway heading north with Leo setting a little more weight on the gas pedal, eager to see what the Da Hwa Factory would have to divulge to him.

"D'you give me permission to open her up?" Leo said with a playful grin as they left the crowded city and came to the wide open highway. Not waiting for that permission, he shifted gear and pushed his sporty little luxury car to the max. Caressing the curves, they motored far out of Hong Kong and within minutes the industrial park was in their view.

"So what building is it?"

"Da Hwa Factory."

Again, Leo tried to act like he knew nothing, but it drove him crazy. How had Peter gotten such information so fast?

"You really think that's where they took her?"

"Absolutely."

"Why Da Hwa? There are so many factories they could choose from."

Peter turned to look straight at him. "What do you think?"

So Peter also knew Da Hwa belonged to him. "Da Hwa is run by Lee Holdings."

"That's right."

"What do you think they're trying to say?"

"Clearly they want to get the message across."

"And what message would that be?"

Peter chuckled. "I told you not to underestimate these guys. They want you to know how easy it is to infiltrate your life, anytime, anywhere, any way. Just like that they can get close to someone you care about... right under your nose and without raising the slightest suspicion. As it stands, there's no way you can tell who's on your side and who's on theirs." Solemn, he looked at Leo. "They're running the show, and they want to make sure you know it. And, police protection or not, they can get to you."

Chapter 11

Zara

Zara awoke to a pounding headache and sore shoulder blades. Opening her eyes to the opaque darkness of the bag still over her head, she instantly remembered her last moments at the hospital and the sudden onset of extreme fatigue.

Struggling to bring relief to her aching arms and shoulders, she realized her wrists were still bound behind her back, the source of the pain between her shoulder blades. Angry with herself for allowing such a thing to happen to her, she tugged even harder in an attempt to free her hands, but it was hopeless.

At the sound of shuffling footsteps approaching her, she ceased all movement, and held her breath as she listened. The footsteps stopped and were followed by the distinct sound of a chair being dragged across the floor.

"Hello, young lady," a mature and authoritative voice said.

Zara turned to the sound of the voice, but refused to respond.

The room was suddenly flooded with light and the darkness of the bag over her head lost a degree of opaqueness, allowing her to make out vague shadows and silhouettes.

"How do you like your new job as Mr. Lee's assistant?"

"I enjoy it very much," she said in a clear and confident voice. No way was she going to even hint at the fear she felt. "Every day is a challenge, but, then again, with my college education and skills, I think I could be doing so much more."

A hearty laugh echoed in the space around her and a chill ran up her spine. It was a sincere laugh, one she might have enjoyed hearing under different circumstances, but under the dark sack on her head, the laughter took on an even darker and more sinister meaning.

"So young," the man said. "So confident. I guess that's how it is for all you new college graduates. You guys think you can just snap your fingers and own the world. A college degree and you think you're capable of running a company, even if you've never set foot in a CEO's office before."

The room fell silent for a long moment and Zara wondered what he was doing. Her ears perked up to capture the slightest sound, but there was nothing.

"Kim, pull that sack off her head, will you?"

Zara stiffened as heavy footsteps came up behind her.

"I want to see the face of the person I'm talking to," the older gentleman added.

A large and heavy hand gripped her shoulder while the other loosened the tie around her neck.

"Easy, you brute," the older man warned. "After all this is a lady, and we should treat her with respect. Be gentle."

The brute responded with a grunt, but softened his hold on Zara's shoulder as he pulled the bag off her head. Instantly blinded by the glaring overhead lights, she squinted and strained to see the face of the man holding her captive, but he remained a blurred silhouette.

"That's better," the man said. "You're quite pleasant to look at."

If he expected her to thank him for the compliment, he'd have to wait a long time.

"So here's the proposition I have for you," he finally said. "I'm impressed by the fact that you've been able to get in so close to Lee, and I'd like to take advantage of your accomplishment. I need you to be close to him, to stay close, and maybe get even closer. I want to know everything about him; every move he makes, every decision he takes, and every plan he puts into effect. I want to know who he trusts, who he confides in. I believe you have the capacity to get all this information without attracting any suspicion whatsoever."

"You want me to spy on Leopold Lee?" Zara said as the man's face became a little clearer.

He laughed with heartfelt amusement, the amusement of a loving grandfather towards a creatively naughty grandchild. "I've never liked the sound of that word; spy. It sounds so hypocritical and harsh."

A numbing sensation crawled over her skin as Zara realized whom she was speaking to. The older voice, slow, steady, confident, articulate... it sounded so much like the voice of the man who would lead a criminal ring, the brutal kind.

"I much prefer to think of it as simply getting to know the man," he added. "Through you."

That inflection... she knew she'd heard that voice before and was increasingly certain of his identity. As pleasant and genteel as his voice sounded, he had the capacity to inflict pain and devastation. A snap of his finger could create such havoc as to make the most horrific medieval war look like child's play.

Through the blur of the blinding lights, she saw him cross his arms over his chest.

"Think of me as a friend, or perhaps an old uncle. I want you to contact me every evening and tell me how your day went. Surely you can do that. It could be a pleasant moment every day where you share what you learned, what you saw, what you heard. You know they say that keeping it all inside can be harmful to your health, so just think of me as your daily dose of anti stress medication."

"You mean gossip."

"Gossip! Yes. Exactly. Every woman loves to gossip, doesn't she?"

Zara grimaced and wanted to tell him what she really thought about his view on women, but kept it to herself.

"Just think of me as your gossip buddy."

There was something disarmingly charming about his manner. Had she been unaware of his true identity, she might have fallen victim to his charm.

"Look," he said. "I'm just an old man. I don't get around much, and I don't know much about what's going on out there. You'll be my eyes and ears. The one who'll regale me with stories of your day."

He made it sound so easy, even attractive.

"I want you to start working for me as of tomorrow morning. You're a bright and capable young woman and I'm sure you'll do a great job of keeping me well informed."

"It sounds a little unethical."

He waved a dismissive hand at her comment. "Every single day, all around the world, people are coming home after a hard day at work and they're venting to their spouse, their friends, their parents about the day's events."

"But…"

"This is a competitive world. Everyone is looking for that edge, the edge that can help them succeed. That's all I want."

His face became clear, and the dark and deep set soulful eyes and crinkled skin reinforced the grandfather figure he seemed to be portraying.

"And consider this," he added. "The information you provide will help me make decisions that can impact thousands of workers, and perhaps millions of citizens. The work you do for me can change lives."

If the old man saw her simply as an assistant he could manipulate, and not the undercover cop she truly was, she could find out what he really intended to do with Leo.

"Okay, so I go to work, I make a mental note of everything I see and hear and I give you a call every night to talk it over."

"That's about it."

"And what do I get out of this arrangement?" she said, playing along with the plan.

"Don't worry. You'll be handsomely rewarded for your efforts.

"All right."

"You're on board?"

"Sure."

"Wonderful," the old man said with a sound clap of his hands. "And now, just to show my good intentions, to show my appreciation, I'm going to contact the hospital and make sure your grandmother is especially well taken care of."

"Oh?"

"Yes, of course. And as long as you're doing a good job, as long as I'm satisfied with the pertinence of the information you're providing, I'll make sure she gets the best treatment possible."

Behind the congenial smile, behind the gruff but warm voice, Zara heard the veiled threat in the promise to take care of her grandmother.

"I have nurses in place who will feed her, wash her, make sure she gets the proper dose of any and all medication, and ensure her overall well-being."

"These nurses are already there?" Her heart pounded as she thought of her vulnerable grandmother. She'd die if anything happened to her because of this job.

He nodded. "In fact, the head nurse works with us; a very cooperative woman."

UNASSUMED

She hoped she hadn't gone as pale as she felt.

"We understand each other?" he said.

"We understand each other," she confirmed with a solemn nod.

Chapter 12

Leo

As they neared the old industrial district that housed Da Hwa and its surrounding housing project, Leo prepared to take the off ramp.

"No," Peter said. "Don't take this exit."

Frowning, Leo looked at him. It'd been a few years since he'd been to Da Hwa, but he could've sworn it'd been at that exit. Then again, he'd never driven there himself. He tried to think back to the last time he'd even come out to the area. Had he been eleven years old? No. He'd been even younger. Surely no older than eight.

A smile slowly came to his lips as he thought of that long ago visit. His father had often spoken of the factory that made rice noodles and Leo had always been curious to see how they were made. His father had finally agreed to bring him along for a visit.

In his boyish and naïve mind, he'd imagined rows of regular kitchen stoves, each with a cook standing behind it stirring pots of boiling water. On entering the fascinating factory, he'd marveled at the immense vats, the automated packaging machines and the rolls and rolls of plastic that were to form the packaging for the individual servings of rice noodles. Spices and flavoring were quickly dropped into tiny envelopes and sealed before being added to the packaging.

"Wow, Father. Everything goes by so fast," he'd told his father who'd simply patted him on the head.

Once in their individual packets, the noodles headed to the shipping department by way of conveyor belts where they were packed into boxes by the dozen. What intrigued Leo, however, was a group of women sitting at a table to the side who randomly took a packet from the conveyor belt and opened it.

"What do they do, Father?"

"Quality control."

"They taste the noodles?" Leo said, his eyes wide with envy. "Can I taste one, too?"

With uncustomary patience, his father led him to the women and offered him a packet of ramen noodles. Like the women at the table, Leo pulled apart the packaging and broke off a piece of noodle to put it in his mouth. Giving the women a nod of approval, he was rewarded with a round of amused laughter.

"When I get big, I'm going to make good food, too," he told the women. His love of food and his desire to see his creations eaten all over the world had begun on that day. Just as so many ramen noodles were to be shipped to America, he wanted to send tasty sauces and spices. And for every packet of rice noodles shipped to Europe, he wanted to send prepared soups and stews, and so much more.

"You'll be running plenty of factories when you grow up," his father said.

"Not only that. I want to be a chef. I want to create foods."

His father chuckled. "Believe me, you'll have plenty to keep you busy just running this factory. Being a boss isn't easy. You have to know what sells, and what doesn't. You have to know which products do well and where. You have to find the best possible ingredients at the lowest possible price in order to keep profits high."

"I want to make good food no matter how much it costs."

"Just remember to charge your customer the difference. In packaged foods, many people are looking to save a buck. They want good taste at a low, low price." His father picked up a packet of seasonings. "See this? The best way to make a few herbs and spices go a long way is to add plenty of salt. Salt cost nothing. Spices can be expensive."

But before Leo could break open the packet of seasonings and lick his finger to dip it inside like he'd seen the women do, his father pulled him away with a firm hand.

Several years after that visit, as a mature teen, Leo had peeked into his father's office, the very office he now called his own.

"Sales are down in America, Europe and Australia," a man said.

"Then again, if you look at the production from Dui Fong, we're having trouble keeping up with the demand," another man said.

"Yes," his father said. His tone was grave, even more so than usual. "I never thought that product line would take off, but…"

"But an increase in health conscience shoppers has made it a hit."

His father nodded, his fingers clasped in front of him. "The success of Dui Fong doesn't make this any easier, but it has to be done. We have to close Da Hwa."

The office fell silent for a long moment, as if the men inside mourned the death of a company, but even then, Leo suspected there was more to the story than just customer preference.

His father's health had declined considerably in the past years and he'd been increasingly absent from the office, leaving major decisions to a handful of trusted men. Leo couldn't help but wonder if those men had been as stringent and diligent in their decision making process as his father had always been.

"I'll start the paperwork and see how many orders we can cancel," the man said.

"Try to cancel as many as possible," his father said. "We're losing money with every order we fill."

It had taken over a year and a half to finally fill the last of orders that would have been too costly to cancel and close the factory, leaving hundreds of employees with no work and no means of feeding their family. That was five years earlier and Leo still felt the sting. Although he'd been in Tibet filming a movie at the time, he'd heard of the closing, the news had been that big. Every paper had talked about the effect on the local economy.

Many had openly blamed his father for his carelessness, callousness and complete lack of empathy when they learned that despite having known of the impending shut down for well over a year, the managers had refused to let the employees know anything until the day they were handed their last paycheck and thanked for their years of loyal dedication.

The press had had a field day with the heartlessness of the company's methods. Distressed by it all, his father had sought to hire back as many employees as possible in other companies under the Lee Holdings umbrella, but he'd been advised against it, and had ultimately followed that advice. Money was growing tight and it wasn't time to be overly charitable.

"Over there," Peter said, breaking Leo from his reverie.

The factory came into view and Leo was flooded with a fresh wave of childhood memories.

"Peter," Leo said. "Why'd they pick Da Hwa factory? I mean, I get how they might want to make a statement, but why go to the trouble of coming all the way out here?" The truth was, Leo wanted to know just how much Peter truly knew about Da Hwa.

"Look around. The place is deserted. We've been driving for over half an hour, and we've barely seen a handful of cars in the last fifteen minutes."

Leo looked around. The small but efficient little town that had been built for the employees of Da Hwa and had thrived for well over twenty years was no longer. The skeleton of many buildings remained upright while others had been completely leveled. "It's a desolate place. For a while there were even rumors the place was cursed."

"All the more appealing to the unsavory crowd, you know what I mean?"

Leo nodded.

"Criminals love to be away from it all when it comes to their dirty business. No witnesses. No one to hear the screams of their victims. No cops around. Nothing. Just pure obscurity and an easy way out."

The appeal of the area's isolation made sense, but there were plenty of faraway places. No, Leo felt certain there was more to the choice of location than that. The more he thought about the life and death of Da Hwa, the more certain he felt the connection between the factory and the criminal ring was an important one.

The leader of the crime ring in France had turned out to be the trusted employee of his victim and had been embezzling for years before finally resorting to kidnapping.

Leo didn't want to suspect one of his father's trusted employees of being so dishonest, but he couldn't afford to be so naïve as to believe it couldn't happen to him. He tapped the back of his steering wheel to activate his hands free mobile phone.

"Ned Liu," Leo called out to his phone.

Startled, Peter looked at him a moment before realizing what he was doing.

The call was put through and the phone rang.

"Liu," Leo said the moment he picked up. "I want you to pull up everything you can find on the Da Hwa factory closing; all press, interviews, news items… everything."

"Yes, sir. Anything else?"

Leo thought a moment. "Do you know who was in charge of Da Hwa at the time it closed down?"

"Hold on…"

The clickety click of computer keys came through the phone.

"All right. Here it is… Horace Su."

"Horace Su?" Leo repeated, trying to put a face to the name.

"Yes, sir. If you're interested to know, it seems he was more than just a manager. If I remember correctly, he was your father's classmate in college and a fellow scientist. In fact, he even helped Lee Holdings branch out into food development and preparation."

"Go on."

"Well, I know he had his own lab at Da Hwa, and this was where he concocted all of the new food items that eventually made it to market. He won a lot of awards for his creations, and many of the products went on to be imitated, but never quite duplicated. He had strict rules when it came to guarding his secret ingredients. He had a knack for making good tasting food at a good price."

UNASSUMED

"So, what happened? Why did Da Hwa ultimately fail if his creations were so in demand and so protected?"

"He grew old, became weak and easily fatigued. He also became increasingly confused. He simply wasn't able to keep up with the continuous new lines of food items other companies were coming up with. Ultimately, he made a costly mistake, insisting a new herb would be the latest health craze, but under closer inspection, the new herb proved to be slightly toxic; not enough to kill anyone, but just enough to sound the alarm to consumers around the world; Da Hwa was potentially poisoning its clients. Everything went downhill after that. Your father had no choice but to fire him."

"How did he take it?"

"Some say he was relieved. He hadn't wanted to let your father down by resigning, but knew he was no longer productive."

"But the factory still closed down."

"It was too late by then. Everything was falling apart and regardless of who took over, the factory was doomed."

"Thanks, Liu. Don't forget to get me everything you can find on the closing."

"Will do."

Leo hung up just as the old factory came into view.

"Turn here," Peter said. "There are no windows along that wall. No one will see us coming."

Leo steered the car where Peter pointed. "Now what?" he said as he parked the car in the shade of the decrepit building.

"Do you know how to fight?"

Leo scoffed at the question. "What kind of a question is that? Of course I can fight."

"This isn't a movie set. This is the real deal."

"Why does everyone keep telling me that? Don't you think I can tell the difference?"

"Honestly? No. I don't think you realize how dangerous it can get out there."

"I'm highly trained in martial arts. It's not just for the camera. I don't have a stuntman who steps in and does all that. It's me."

"Yes, it's you, but the bad guys are just actors who are told to be careful not to hurt you all while making it look as if they're kicking your ass."

"Just get out of the car, will you?" Leo opened the door and got out, eager to show the uppity cop just what he was made of.

Peter came up beside him and they headed to the main entrance of the factory.

"Stay close," Peter said as he pulled out a gun. "And don't get any fancy ideas of playing the hero. I don't want the blood of the heir to Lee Holdings on my hands."

"I'll do my best not to get killed on your watch," Leo said with a sarcastic smirk. "Lord knows I wouldn't want my death to tarnish your impeccable reputation."

"You're lucky I let you come out here at all. I should have left you at the hospital."

Leo tried to stay calm, but grew increasingly irritated by Peter's condescending manner. "There's no way in hell you could have kept me from coming. I'm here to save Zara, and I'll do whatever it takes." He turned to look directly at Peter. "What I've inherited has no bearing on what I'm willing to do for her."

Peter stopped and turned to him. "So. I was right."

"Right about what?"

"You. You and Zara . You have the hots for her, don't you?"

"What business is that of yours?"

"Don't sidestep the question, and don't deny it. I've seen that look that comes over you every time I mention her name."

"Yeah, right."

"Admit it. You want her. You crave her. You'll do anything to have her." A look akin to jealousy took over his features for a fraction of a second before the professional police officer returned. "Well, you'd better get in line, because you're not the first."

"You mean you?"

Peter took a half step close, but stopped himself and backed away. "She's taken. I didn't spend three years at the Hong Kong police force for nothing. Just keep that in mind."

They'd reached the side entry, and Peter put a cautionary hand out in front of Leo. "Focus. This could get ugly fast. Our main objective is to get Zara out safely. We'll deal with whoever's behind this once she's out of danger."

"Thanks for making that clear," Leo quipped. "I thought we'd just stepped out to stretch our legs."

"Stop playing the wise guy," Peter said. "This is…"

Just as Peter fell silent, Leo caught an abrupt movement from the corner of his eye and turned to see a man in a black windbreaker and jeans jump on Peter, knocking him to the ground.

Peter struggled as the man tried to grab his gun.

While Peter dealt with the assailant, Leo ran into the factory, eager to find Zara. Inside he spotted a limp figure sitting in a darkened corner of the room. Even through the gloom, he knew it was Zara. Seeing her in that chair, her head hung long and her hair obscuring her face, Leo immediately feared he was too late.

His heart clenched at the thought any harm had come to her because of him.

"Zara," he whispered as he hurried beside her, brushing her hair out of her face. "Oh, my God, Zara. Please…"

She groaned and feebly raised her head. "Wha…?"

"Zara." Peter ran his hand over her cheek.

178

"Leo. How d'you…?"

He silenced her with a kiss, a kiss he'd been thinking of since meeting her at the hospital that morning. He savored her sweet lips and tasted her tongue, aroused by the slow dance their mouths embarked on.

With difficulty, he pulled back and reached back to find her wrists were tightly bound. "We've got to get you out of here."

A gunshot rang out, quickly followed by a heavy and sickening thud. Seconds later, the door opened and Peter ran in, his smoking gun still in his hand. It took him a moment to assess the situation, but once he saw Zara, he ran to her, efficiently shoving Leo aside.

"Zara, are you all right?" He quickly worked to free her wrists. "Did you see who did this to you? Do you know where they are?"

Before she could answer a single question, he pulled her out of the chair and into his arms. His lips clasped over hers and his hands ran up her back, squeezing her to him. "I knew I'd find you," he said as he dropped a series of tender kisses along her temple.

He sensually massaged her shoulders then brought his hands to her wrists, rubbing them with loving care.

Stunned by the spectacle, Leo stared at the couple in disbelief. He'd suspected something between Peter and Zara, but hadn't really expected such passion between the two.

Adding to his astonishment was seeing Zara completely give herself to Peter. He wanted to see her fight Peter off, ask him what the hell he was doing, who the hell he thought he was. He wanted her to disentangle herself from his hold and come running to him. Instead, she kissed Peter back.

It's Peter who finally pulled away from her. "Don't ever pull a stunt like this again," he said in a reprimanding tone. "I know how much you want to get the guys behind all this... I know you want to get your hands on the men who killed your parents, but..."

Leo stared at Peter then turned a confused look to Zara. She'd never mentioned her parents' death was connected to this crime ring.

"I know how important this case is to you, but I want you to remember just how important you are to me." Peter pulled her closer to him, his hands sliding down to her ass and pulling her into his crotch. "Baby, when this whole thing is over..." He bit down hungrily on his bottom lip. "I can't wait to settle down with you, to have you in my arms every night. The sooner we get this case solved, the better."

She pulled back to look up at him, and Peter quickly snatched her lips with his, covering her mouth in a hungry kiss which she greedily returned.

Leo wanted to retch. He was in shock. So she really was involved with Peter. Peter said they were practically engaged. But how could she have reacted to his moves on her the way she did? Leo wanted to believe it was because women have always found him irresistible, but with Zara, he wanted it to be real. It had to be real. She wasn't an actress nor a model who wanted to use him to get into acting. Her body's reaction to him was real, and he knew despite her current display of affection for Peter, she was still attracted to him no matter what.

He watched as Peter's hands rubbed and squeezed Zara's ass in a sensual mix of bringing back circulation to her lower bottom, while he kissed her. Leo's hands clenched. He wanted to be the one holding Zara and molding her ass to his crotch. No longer able to stand the sight of the loving couple, he turned to inspect the factory his father had once run with such a tight and expert hand.

But his eyes were blind to everything around him. All he could see was Zara in Peter's arms.

He was relieved to find her alright, but felt awful. Why had she allowed him to kiss her when he'd found her. She hadn't fought him off, had never mentioned another man in her life.

Could she be that good at playing the role assigned to her? He'd asked her to be the candy on his arm, and she'd dutifully obliged... heated kisses and all. Or did she have any feelings for him. Anything at all?

Damn it.

No matter how he looked at the situation, he felt like crap. He had never felt so dejected by a woman. He had never wanted a woman as much as he wanted Zara.

Chapter 13

Leo

Leo walked aimlessly through the factory that was so still and silent. He could still remember the purr of the automated packing machines. It'd been a deafening purr.

Turning into a corridor, he headed to the laboratory, the part of the factory that had impressed him the most. So many innovative products had been concocted in the large, white and sterile room.

The door was ajar and he peered into the room, surprised by how dusty and rundown it seemed, but when he went to push the door open wider, he stopped at the sound of voices.

Male voices came from inside the laboratory and Leo suddenly realized they were still in danger. How could he have been so blinded by Peter and Zara's tender embrace that he'd ignored the possible danger that still surrounded them?

UNASSUMED

Two men stood by the window, their silhouettes backlit by the strong sunlight that streamed in, but aside from the silhouettes, Leo could make out no features whatsoever. Even more frustrating, he couldn't make out what they were saying.

Why had they not come running at the sound of the gunshot? he wondered.

The answer came to him quickly enough. The walls of the laboratory were thick and well insulated.

Concentrating, he tried to put a face to one of the voices. Though muffled, he could make out the distinctly gruff and authoritative tone of an older, more mature man.

He'd heard that voice before, but his foggy, boyhood memory refused to cooperated and give him any clues as to who it could be.

Backing up against the wall, Leo looked around for any sign of other thugs in the factory. Before he made a move, he had to make sure he was alone. Once certain, he doubled back and headed back to Peter and Zara, determined to break up their loving embrace once and for all.

He was almost at the corridor that would lead him to them when a strong hand came down hard over his shoulder. Without bothering to turn to see who it was, he rammed a heavy elbow into the assailant's gut and turned around to see a large man stumble back.

"What the hell?" Leo said.

The big man answered him by pulling out a sword and waving it in Leo's face. A large silly grin came over the man's face. "Leo Lee. I'm a big fan."

Right, Leo thought.

"I've always admired those moves of yours." He tossed the blade into his other hand and back again. "Now let's see what kind of kung fu moves you have in real life."

Circling Leo, the big man deftly swung the sword up and around, then took a swift leap at him, ready to lop off Leo's head.

Snickering at the foreseeable move, Leo leaned back to avoid the blade, his back low and parallel to the floor. Grateful he'd kept limber and flexible the past years, he straightened up and grinned. Had he neglected to stay in shape, his head would be rolling on the floor.

"Cool move," the big man said. "But you're going to run out of cool moves before I'm through with you."

185

UNASSUMED

Leo knew he was right. He needed to get his hand on a weapon, or get the hell out of there. With no possibility of finding a weapon, he opted to run, hoping the big man would prove unable to move quickly, but the big guy was swift and quickly had Leo up against the wall.

While the man raised the sword high above his head and prepared to bring it down on him, Leo reached for a nearby rusted baking sheet and held it up as a shield. With a clang, the blade came down on the baking sheet, denting it, but saving Leo from the cutting blow.

Leo dashed out from under the man, throwing the baking sheet at his head as he ran.

"You can run, but there's not much place to hide, movie star. Where you gonna go to when you don't have a director telling you what to do? Huh? Can you think for yourself, little rich boy?"

Running at full speed, Leo turned abruptly and headed towards the big man, zigzagged at the last second, ran a few steps up the wall behind him and flipped up into the air, coming down on the man from an angle that completely caught him off guard. With a solid punch to the jaw and Leo's fingers drilling into his eyes, blinding him for life, the man fell to the floor screaming in pain.

"How's that for a cool move?" Leo said as he landed on his feet and looked down at this handiwork.

Rubbing his bloodied eyes with his massive hand, the man remained on all fours as he groaned and cursed.

Leo turned to head back to Peter and Zara, but the distinct whizzing sound of metal slicing through the air made him turn back in time to see the sword flying towards him. Moving aside just in time to see the sword embed itself in the wall behind him, Leo was stunned when he heard a gunshot.

"Peter," Zara called out.

Leo turned to pair who'd quickly run up to the fallen man.

"What have you done?" Zara said to Peter.

Leo came up behind them. Disgusted by the sight of the man's blown out face, he quickly turned away.

"I had to do it, baby," Peter said. "You saw the man. He tried to slice Leo's head off."

"But..."

"I did what I had to do to protect the heir to Lee Holdings. I had no other choice. He's the last one left and we have to ensure his safety."

Zara sighed as she looked down at the dead man. "You're right," she finally said. "You had no choice."

"Come on, you two," Peter said. "There's nothing else to do here. I'll call ahead to have the two bodies taken in and the place swept."

"You should've never come out here on your own to begin with," Zara said as she walked beside Peter, Leo lagging behind. "How come you didn't call for back up?"

"It all happened so fast. I just wanted to get out here as quickly as possible."

"Well, you could've been hurt, but I'm glad you made it here fast enough."

"And now it's time to take you home, get you into a nice hot shower and then out for a great dinner."

"Peter," Zara said. "I told you earlier. I'm not ready for that yet."

"Not ready for a shower and a good hot meal? Come on."

"I know very well that's not all you have in mind."

"Okay, so I want to show you just how much I love you. Damn it, even filthy and disheveled you are the most beautiful and amazing women to me, Zara." He came to an abrupt stop, pulled Zara into his arms and smothered her with a hungry kiss.

Grinding his teeth, Leo took a good look at the pair for a sickening moment before walking past them. Peter was rubbing it in. So he'd gotten the girl. Good for him. No need to make a show of it.

As he exited the old factory, he remembered the man he really was; the heir to billions and a sexy and talented movie star. He could have any woman he desired. Zara wasn't the only hot woman in Hong Kong, and it was time he put the detective out of his mind and get back to what he did best; casual flings that involved a lot of hot sex with no strings at all.

Chapter 14

Leo

Stepping out of the old factory, Leo stopped to look around the old ghost town. He knew he was stalling. While every ounce of testosterone told him to move on and find a sexy body to vent all his frustrations on, something held him back.

Nostalgia, he tried to tell himself. Being at Da Hwa made him feel closer to his father, but that was a lie, just a pretense to remain standing there thinking and feeling… all for Zara.

She'd been shadowing him for weeks, and he ought to be relieved to have her off his back. He could return to his real life, the life he'd always loved. But he had to admit, she'd grown on him, and fast. He felt safe and secure around her, but not because of her ability to protect him. It was a certain emotional safety he'd found with her. He could just be himself around her and that had been worth all the money in the world.

In the distance he saw the whirr of red and blue lights from two police cruisers. That was fast, he thought. Might as well stick around to see if he could learn anything new about the assailants.

The police cruisers came to an abrupt stop right in front of him, and four officers stepped out as if performing a well-choreographed dance. They came around the front of the cars, all four of them looking at Leo.

"They're still in there," Leo said pointing to the door that led to the loving couple.

But he needn't have pointed it out. Peter and Zara emerged from the building and spoke briefly to one of the officers while the others went inside.

"I've got to hurry back into town to write up a report," Peter said, his hand discreetly caressing the small of Zara's back. "I'll drop you off at the clinic," he told her.

"I'm fine."

He glared at her.

"Fine. I'll go." She turned to follow him to one of the cruisers. "But I know I'm fine."

"Ty," Peter called out. "We're going to hitch a ride back into town with you."

UNASSUMED

The young officer who'd just come out of the building stopped to confer with his superior then headed to the car. Zara didn't look back at Leo as the young officer started the car, backed up and sped away. He was all but forgotten.

Well, he'd have to do what was necessary to forget all about her. Never mind how sexy and alive she was. Never mind how she turned him on without even trying. Never mind that he thought his world had changed forever just by knowing her.

Never mind how the thought of her in Peter's arms almost drove him to insanity.

He sat at the wheel of his expensive little sports car, pulled out his smart phone and pulled up all his female contacts. Surely there was a woman who could rid him of all the frustrations Zara had left him with.

"Vanessa," he murmured.

They'd met as teens back when her father, Bohai See, had been his father's partner. She'd been an awkward teen with long skinny limbs, breasts smaller than his own and teeth that desperately needed work, but the photo she'd put on her social media pages showed a whole new girl; silicon breasts that were large and round like melons, perfectly aligned teeth that sparkled brilliantly white. All of the awkwardness of her teen years was gone, thanks to surgery, as displayed in a photo of her lying back in bed with her stiletto clad feet up in the air to better show the perfect fit of her lace panties.

"I guess you'll do," he said with a smirk.

Although Bohai See had moved on from Lee Holdings and now ran one of the top conglomerates in the country, Vanessa had retained her reputation as a wild child and she didn't shy away from sharing her exploits with the world of social media. Photos of her drinking the night away competed with photos of her new sexy body clad in as little clothing as was legally allowed.

She was exactly what he needed. Mindless sex.

He looked further into her background and her past times. A page was dedicated to her favorite past time; sex. The page boasted photos she'd posted of herself with various men, many of them in scandalous positions. It was a veritable who's who of wealthy young bachelors in Hong Kong, and she'd been pestering Leo for months to join that list. Being who he was, he was sure she wanted him as much as he wanted her…purely physical, and for her, another notch on her bedpost.

Pride had kept him from joining at first, and then he'd met Zara, and all thoughts of Vanessa had faded away, but now… he dialed her up.

"Vanessa, what are you up to?"

Recognizing him, she groaned deep in her throat before her helium-balloon high voice said, "I thought you'd never ask."

"How about dinner tonight? Let's say the Qi Quon Qiang Inn at eight o'clock.

She squealed with delight, a piercing and persistent sound that forced Leo to pull the phone away from his ear.

"I'll take that as a yes." He brought the phone back to his ear. "We'll have dinner in my favorite suite."

"Oh," she squealed again.

"See you then." He put the phone away, happy with the step he'd taken to permanently put Zara out of his mind, and started his car.

*****

Leo wore the sleek black suit that made him feel alive again. It fit his body perfectly, and he loved the luxurious feel of the expensive garments. It was good to be back to his old ways, and when he answered the knock at the door and saw Vanessa, he knew he was in for a good time.

Wearing a red floor length gown that was slit up to her pelvic bone and cut strategically low between her enormous breasts, she was the perfect uber rich slut, ready to do anything to please a man.

"How do you like it?" she said as she turned her backside to him. The back of the dress was just as sparse as the front.

It was a little too tacky for his taste, but the sexual effect on his cock was undeniable. Wild sex was on the menu and he couldn't wait to dig in.

"Come in," he said. "I was just opening a bottle of champagne."

She sashayed in and immediately made herself comfortable on the pristine white leather sofa. She didn't even glance at the dining table that was elegantly set with fine china and glimmering silver.

Leo poured champagne into two flutes and joined her.

"Thanks." She took the champagne flute, tapped it to his and gulped back the contents before setting it aside. "I love the good stuff,"

"I've had a sumptuous dinner prepared for us."

She ran her hand over his lap and reached for the zipper on his pants. "You're all the dinner I need."

"Hang on." Leo took her hand. "We have all night."

"Don't worry, baby. I plan on keeping you busy all night, and then some." She kicked a tanned and toned leg up and draped it over his knee while her hand resumed its quest for freeing his member, rubbing and massaging her fingers all over it through the expensive fabric of his pants.

"I thought we'd build up the sexual desire slowly."

"Honey," she said matter-of-factly. "I've been dreaming of this for years. Believe me. Sexual desire is at its ultimate high." She unbuckled his belt, unzipped his pants and pulled his engorged cock out. "And judging by the size of your love machine here, your sexual desire is right up there with mine."

She leaned into him and brought her face to his crotch. Just the thought of what was coming nearly had him exploding. Running her tongue over the length, she moaned and sighed before swallowing it whole into her mouth.

Leo's eyes rolled back as she deep throat him.

"Damn you smell and taste great," she said, "And you're so wide and long..."

Setting his champagne down before he lost his grip on the delicate crystal flute, Leo leaned back and let Vanessa take over. She licked him again and again, as she brought her mouth up and down his shaft before taking him all into her heated mouth.

"Oh, my God," Leo let out.

She sucked on him with practiced precision, putting just enough pressure as she pulled him in, and just enough suction when she pulled back.

"Where'd you learn to do that?"

"I'd be lying if I said you were my first," she said with a sensual smile as she sat up and looked at him. Arching her back, she thrust her bust at him. "I didn't have all this work done just to fill out a bikini. These girls have been hard at work attracting attention, mesmerizing men and... well, you'll just have to wait and see."

UNASSUMED

Leo pulled his aching and swollen shaft back into his pants, and tried to regain control of the situation. "So how come a great catch like yourself isn't engaged or married yet?"

"Oh, please. I've spent the last few years fucking the brains out of virtually every hot and rich guy around, but do you really think I have what it takes to make for a good wife? I mean, look at me. I'm not exactly socialite material."

"Aren't you underestimating yourself?"

"Don't feel sorry for me, Leo. I'm having the time of my life. I have more fun than any of those men's wives. I mean, how dull must it be to have to prepare crustless finger sandwiches for a bunch of blue haired hags?"

Leo winced. "That's pretty rough."

"Hey, life's rough. You gotta get your kicks where you can." She stood and pulled the panel of her dress back to expose her bare crotch. "Speaking of which…"

Leo's cock throbbed with the need to feel her lips around him again, but instead of reaching for him, Vanessa ran her fingers over herself and moaned.

"I am so wet and ready for you, you have no idea. You're even sexier than I remember. So hard, so muscular, so perfect, I can barely believe it. You have the best body out of all the men I've ever fucked."

Straddling him, Vanessa thrust her breasts into his face and nestled her warm crotch over his erection. "I'm going to ride you all night long, Leo. You have no idea how long I've dreamed of having you in me...since we first met. I've had the biggest crush on you as a teen, but you were far too pretty and popular for me," Vanessa said, "but not tonight." She slipped himself in her and grinded on top of him like a professional dancer, rotating her hips while moving back and forth in a steady and quick motion.

Through the fuzz of arousal, Leo heard a knock at the door, but his body refused to respond to it. He sighed and let Vanessa's movements over his cock bring him to the brink of exploding.

But the knocking at the door became insistent and the determined pounding finally proved impossible to ignore. "I'd better get that," Leo said as he gripped Vanessa's hips and stopped her sensual motions.

"Seriously?"

He firmly lifted her off him and set her on the sofa beside him, pulling up his pants and tugging his shirt back in as he got up. "I've ordered a few things for dinner."

"Oh, and maybe some dessert, too?"

Smirking, he headed to the door. "Maybe. Management knows I'm here and they've been known to surprise me with specialty items before."

He pulled the bolt on the door, unhooked the chain and pulled the door back, but instead of facing room service, he was faced by a large uniformed man. A delivery? Leo thought, trying to remember if he'd ordered anything other than dinner. "Are you married? Seeing someone, Vanessa?" Leo turned to ask her. "Because there's a man out here who I have no idea..."

"Step back," the man said as he pulled his coat back to show the gun in his belt.

Cursing his negligence, Leo took a step back. Vanessa had gotten him so horny, he hadn't even thought to check the peephole before opening the door. Such a novice mistake, one that could end up costing him his life.

"Leo?" Vanessa called from behind him. "Is everything all right?"

Distracted by Vanessa's exposed breasts and wanton posture, the armed man turned to her just long enough to allow Leo to land a solid kick in the man's chest. The man doubled back as he grabbed his gun and fired, blasting a hole in the ceiling and another shot at the large paned window.

More quickly than Leo had expected, the man regained his balance and raised his arm to aim the gun at him, but Leo whipped his leg back and kicked the gun from his hand.

"Leo!" Vanessa screamed. "Oh, my God! Leo!"

The assailant lunged at Leo who deftly sidestepped him, but the big man turned around, fists flying.

"Leo! Watch out!"

Her distracting screams were all it took to tear Leo's eyes from the man who took advantage of the situation and punched Leo square on the jaw, sending him flying back.

"Oh, no. Leo, he's going to hurt you. Oh, don't let him hurt you," Vanessa's impossibly high-pitched voice screamed, hurting Leo's ears. She should've worked on her voice all these years instead of getting rounds and rounds of plastic surgery. He remembered now why he couldn't stand to talk to her much over the years. Her voice grated on his ears. It was like listening to chipmunks talk to you excitedly all day long.

"If you could just shut up," he muttered under his breath as he struggled to get back to his feet, "I'll be able to manage just fine."

But the man had some explosive fighting skills and he matched Leo's thrusts, punches and kicks time and again. After taking a strong blow to the abdomen, Leo doubled over, allowing his attacker to deliver a crippling kick to his chest.

Breathless and dizzy, Leo looked up as the glimmer of a shining blade came down toward him. The blade stopped in midair, just inches from Leo's neck and for a strangely silent moment, he wondered what was keeping the man from finishing the job. But then he saw the strong but elegant fingers wrapped around his wrists and followed the line of a strong, but decidedly feminine arm until he came to her face.

Zara.

She twisted the man's arm behind his back, twisted his wrist up just enough to force him to drop the knife and kicked it out of reach.

Leo remained on his back and simply stared at her. She was a vision, a beautiful feline, all elongated muscles encased in tight black jeans, a form fitting black t-shirt and sexy killer boots. Her shiny beautiful hair tied back into a ponytail made her look both hot and elegant at the same time. Her movements were as graceful as any ballerina as she brought the big man to his knees, but the strength in her every movement was undeniably lethal.

"Damn, you're hot," Leo couldn't help but say.

"Save it," she shot out.

Just then, the goon at her feet rose, and butted his head back, hitting the back of his head sharply against her nose. Reeling, she stepped back, her eyes glazed over as she put her hands up to her nose.

Leo shot to his feet to settle the fight, but Zara recovered quickly, she managed to get a hold of the man and deliver a swift kick that sent him flying up against the wall right beside Leo.

"Watch out," Zara shouted.

UNASSUMED

Leo turned in time to see the man pull out a smaller knife and hold it up over him for a brief second before driving the small blade into Leo's shoulder. Stunned by the pain, he let out an agonized gasp and tried to move before the man could deliver another blow, but once again the blade found its mark, driving deep in the flesh of his upper arm.

Zara reached him before he could deliver a third blow, but the man refused to give in so easily. He slapped his hand back, landing the large, sharply honed ring on his middle finger right above her left eye. She faltered for a moment and wiped the back of her hand across the side of her face. Seeing the blood on her hand, she glared up at the goon.

"Didn't your mother ever teach you not to play with sharp objects in the house?" She swung around and brought her leg back under his, effectively kicking his legs out from under him. He fell back allowing Zara to deliver a few sharp blows, but it was almost as if he were humoring her, for when he'd had enough, he got to his feet and fought her with all that he had.

Blow for blow, kick for kick, they battled it out with the same degree of expertise. He seemed to know every trick she had and often foresaw her next move.

"You've got some pretty moves, little lady," he growled.

"Little lady? I'll show you some pretty moves." She took two steps towards him, jumped in the air with her feet out in front of her, and caught the heel of her boot in the man's cheek. He flew back and fell to the floor, his face oozing blood.

She reached to her back pocket to pull out the handcuffs, but the man wasn't through.

"You're not going to take me in that easily. I've got a job to do and I'm going to get it done, or die trying."

"Your call."

He blasted his way to her, kicking her knees down and while she fell to the floor, he jumped up, ran to get his fallen gun and fired a shot at Leo. He missed, giving Zara the chance to get to her feet and run to Leo.

Another shot rang out just as Zara came to stand in front of Leo, effectively guarding him with her life.

"No," Leo shouted as he tried to push her out of the way, but it was too late. A shot rang out. "Zara !"

UNASSUMED

She closed her eyes and for a terrifying moment, he thought he'd lost her, but it was the big man who hit the floor with a deafening thud, his dead eyes staring into nothingness.

"Looks like I've just saved your arse again," Peter said as he blew a satisfactory breath to the tip of his smoking gun. He calmly walked to the assailant's side and kicked the gun away. "I think he's done."

"He's dead?" Zara said, "but I wanted to question him."

After placing the man's gun in a plastic bag, he knelt beside Zara, pulling her into his arms. "Yes, he's dead, and you've once again scared me to death."

"Peter, we needed that man's testimony. Who knows what information he might have had?"

"All the information in the world would mean nothing if you were dead, which is what would have happened had I not arrived in time." Peter turned a resolved glance to Leo. "Once again, I've saved you from certain death."

Chapter 15

Zara

Zara tried to ignore the pain in her knee and made her way to the assassin's body to go through his pockets. "There must be something in here that can give us a clue as to who he is." But there was nothing; no identification, no notes, no cards of any kind. Nothing. "A big fat blank."

"What d'you expect? These guys are pros."

She turned her attention to the man's weapons. "This guy isn't with the ring."

"What makes you say that?"

"Look at this gun. The guys back at Da Hwa all had glocks and AK47s. This guy is going around with a small revolver." She didn't want to believe the man was working on his own, but it seemed unlikely he was part of the ring.

With impressive speed and efficiency, Zara took the man's prints, a snapshot of his face, via her smart phone, and sent the information to the precinct. "We'll get this guy checked out."

"And the boys are going to have to come pick up another body." Peter gave the dead man a light nudge in the leg.

Moments later, Zara's phone chimed and she checked her messages. "Hmm," she said, more to herself then the guys. "That's funny."

"What?" Leo said.

She frowned as she continued to stare at the screen of her phone.

"Honey." Peter came to her side and put his arm to her shoulder. "What is it?"

"This man is from Shantou."

"Then why did he come here?" Leo said.

Peter shot an annoyed glance at Leo then back at Zara. "What's in Shantou?"

Still staring at her phone, Zara said, "My parents and I lived just outside Shantou when I was little."

"Oh?"

"That's where they were killed, Peter."

"Why would the people who killed your parents want to kill me?" Leo said.

Zara shrugged. How was it all connected? Or was it simply a coincidence and there was no connection? She didn't really believe in coincidences and her gut told her there was a lot more to discover about the crime ring.

"This is too wild for me. I'm getting out of here."

Zara turned to the sound of the sultry feminine voice. With all the excitement she hadn't noticed the vibrantly dressed sex kitten who now swayed her hips past them to the door.

"Hold on a minute." Peter put a hand to Vanessa's shoulder and shot a quizzical glance at Zara. "Seems our loverboy wasn't alone tonight."

Zara tried to hide her dismay. Not that she expected Leo to be a saint, but to be with such an obviously loose woman... It just seemed so beneath him.

"I think I might have a few questions for you, young lady," Peter said. "As a witness, you could be of help... Miss..."

Vanessa turned away and looked at the floor. "You can call me Nessi."

UNASSUMED

Aside from being dressed for a wild night of sex, there was something about Nessi that Zara didn't appreciate.

Jealous, she told herself. You're being silly and jealous like an immature teenager. Jealous or not, she turned to tend to Leo's wounds. "Did you call for an ambulance, Pete?"

"On their way."

"I'm fine," Leo said.

"Haven't I heard that before?" Her tone was professional and firm. "How are you holding up?"

"I've had better days."

"I'm here to protect you, Leo. You had no business pulling me out of the way like that."

He winced as he tried to sit upright. "You think I could just sit back and let you take a bullet for me?"

She somehow managed to keep a cold and hard exterior as she inspected his wounds. The bullet had caused just a shallow nick that would probably required little more than a Band-Aid, and the stab wounds weren't life threatening. Looking at him, she couldn't believe what he'd done. For a man who had everything, who was seen as a spoiled billionaire who'd come into so much money so easily, he was as selfless as a saint.

She leaned in closer and pulled back his shirt to take a better look at his shoulder. His breath brushed against her skin and she could almost taste the sweetness of his kiss. All too aware of Nessi and Peter standing nearby, she suddenly felt flushed as lurid thoughts of Leo played out in her mind.

"Come on." She helped him up. "We'll go try to wash all this blood off."

As she led him to the bathroom she thought how wonderful it would be to erase whatever thoughts he might have of the sex bomb he'd been planning on spending his night with. How wonderful it would be to lose herself in his embrace, in his kiss... to share his bed, to wake up in this magnificent hotel room and have breakfast with him... to laugh and talk, or just sit back to watch a movie... maybe even one of his movies. She could laugh at him and tease him, tell him where his moves were impossible, or incorrect.

It was all such a blissful dream, one she'd never dared dream.

"You know, I'd pull you out of the way all over again if it meant saving you," Leo said. He ran his hand over her cheek and pulled up to kiss her. "I'd do it all again," he whispered. His kiss was long and deep, drawing her in and making her blissful dream seem so possible, so probable, so within reach. "I'm not letting you go," he said as he looked into her eyes with such intensity, she knew he'd do anything to make her forget Peter.

The sensations that spilled over her were overwhelming and she wanted to abandon all decorum and simply give herself to the passionate kiss. "We've been through this before, Leo. I'm here to..."

"Protect me, yes. I know." Knowledge of her role didn't stop him, however. He pulled her in for another smoldering kiss. And it was heavenly. His soft lips made her heady, and his tongue drew electric shocks from way down between her thighs.

"Leo," she sighed. "I can't."

"If you're so hell-bent on protecting me, why don't you protect me from a broken heart?"

Smiling, she looked at him. You're adorable, she wanted to say. But while she remained silent, her hands did a whole lot of talking. They roamed over his hard muscular body and one finally came to rest over the front of his pants.

"I want you," Leo said. "I can't help it, Zara."

And, damn, I want you, but... Zara bit her lip and looked at the man who had her so perpetually confused. "I think I heard the guys arrive. I'd better go see what's going on."

He gripped her hand as she pulled away. "Stop looking at me as if I were just some spoiled little rich boy who can't take care of himself in the real world. I'm a real man, Zara, and I'm more than a bank account."

Pressing her lips tight, she nodded. It was unfair to think he was just an empty headed heir, but she knew he had a reputation for running around and the woman in the red dress was proof of that.

"I don't think I'm the kind of woman you'd really fall for," she said with a quick glance over her shoulder. "I'm not that wild flash of overt sexuality, and I can't see myself becoming involved with a man who can't take a relationship seriously." She turned away before he could say anything more.

"What's going on?" Zara came up behind Peter.

He turned to scrutinize her. "Maybe I should be asking you that question."

"I thought I heard the guys arrive."

"They're checking the body." He glanced over Zara's shoulder and grimaced.

Guilt was a difficult pill to swallow and the rush of passion that Leo had ignited now made her feel she'd done something wrong. Following Peter's gaze, she turned to see Leo head towards them, a victorious grin on his tired face.

"I want to see you in my office the minute this is over," Peter said, his tone decisive and possessive.

Chapter 16

Zara

"You'll be safe here," Zara told Leo as she patted his hand. The nurse had just left after stitching up his knife wounds. "You'll have two guards at your door at all times."

"I still don't understand why I have to stay here."

"You lost a lot of blood, Leo. Give yourself a chance to recover." She gave his hand a final pat. "I've got to go."

She left him and hurried back to the precinct to report to Peter. More nervous than she'd been in a long time, she knocked lightly on his door and walked in.

"Sit down." He didn't look up from the files on his desk as he gave the order in a cool and distant tone. "And close the door."

Feeling like a reprimanded child, she quietly shut the door and sat down in the chair facing him.

"Today's been a long and difficult day." Peter closed the file on his desk and rose to come pace behind her. "You put yourself in unnecessary danger, again."

"I'm sorry. You know how it is when you're in the heat of the action."

He put his hands on her shoulders and squeezed. "I can't stop thinking of you, Zara." His fingers reached down over her collar bone as if seeking comfort and warmth.

"Peter."

"I can't stand the thought of losing you. I don't know what I'd do. I'd kill any man who'd try to hurt you."

She sat silently examining his words. Were they just an expression of his true fears, or a veiled threat? "I have a job to do, Peter. All I'm trying to do is my job."

Peter suddenly came around in front of her and pulled her out of the chair and into his arms. "I'm so sick with worry about you, that I can't do mine. That man at the hotel...the one who nearly killed you...I shot him dead because he was going to kill you. I could've aimed for his shoulders, shoot his hand...but when I saw him aimed his gun at you and was pulling back the trigger, all I can do was shoot to kill."

Peter ran a hand through his hair. "Zara, I stood by you for three years since I first met you, since I first fell in love with you at first sight. Instead of moving to another division, which I was supposed to do, or head back to England, I stayed in ours…because I had to be around to protect you. To take care of you." He smiled. "You're such a devoted and headstrong officer, without any care in the world for yourself, someone's got to watch out for you. That's why I stayed and even moved up the ranks to become your superior. So I can be on top of all your cases. But now… with Lee's case being so complicated, and I…I am letting my personal feelings interfere with the case. Zara," Peter said gently.

"What Peter," Zara said, looking directly at him. Peter had always been her friend, colleague, and now something more.

Peter said, "I need you to get off this case."

"You know I can't do that."

"Maybe this will convince you." He pulled her in for an intense kiss that left her breathless. His entire body melted into hers, and the bulge in his pants pressed against her. "I want you to come back to England with me."

"What?" she whispered breathlessly, still riding on the heat of his kiss.

"I love you, Zara. I love you more than anything, and I want to spend my life with you." He grasped her hands and held them in the warmth of his, his thumbs running over her skin. "I know this case is important to you, and believe me, I'll do all I can to make sure the people responsible for your parents' death are caught, convicted and punished, but, Zara …" His eyes misted over. "You've become negligent and careless. I think you've become increasingly blinded by your need to solve this case that you overlook the danger you're putting yourself in."

Realizing he was right, she nodded. "I'll be more careful. I promise."

"That's not enough. I want you off this case. Zara, I'll solve this case and then we'll put all this behind us. You'll love life in England. We can live on one of my family's estates, and we can go horseback riding on the estate, host parties…whatever you want, but at least safe with me. But, honey, we'll never know how good life could be if you're not around."

"Peter, you're making me dizzy."

"Did I tell you that I'm to inherit that country cottage? I'm no Leo, but my family have land and my father's has a prestigious and respectable career in government. We'll have a gorgeous flat in the heart of London and that beautiful country cottage for weekend getaways."

"You're moving too fast, Peter. I'm not ready to think about the future yet."

"I've already made plans to step into my father's shoes back home; I'll be the new liaison between Britain and Hong Kong, and you'll be my beautiful wife. Honey, it'll be so magnificent."

The warmth of his hands was so reassuring, but something about his vision of their future together didn't mesh.

"Do you care about me, Zara?" He brought his hands to her temples and pushed them through her hair.

"You know I do." She closed her eyes and let out a pleasurable sigh.

"I can't wait to have you. I can't wait to show you just how much I love you. You'll know what it is to be loved, to be so desired, to be cherished." He planted a long, hard kiss on her lips. "Three years of waiting for you, of being in love with you, Zara...I... desperately... want... you." He pressed up against her, confirming his desire.

She couldn't deny her affection for him built up over the years, too, how he was always there as a friend and colleague, and then last year when he began acting more than a friend, she found that she had always found him handsome and attractive. They were already close as colleagues, and she often shared her hopes and dreams with him, even insecurities.

When he kissed her, she kissed him back, and then let out a surprisingly loud sigh when he brought his hand up under her shirt to her breast. His fingers slipped under the delicate lace of her bra and perked her nipple to life.

"Do you want it?" he groaned into her ear.

She could just sigh as she let her head fall back.

Peter pushed her back to his desk and cleared the piles of paper from it before nudging her up. "Yes," he said as he thrust his cock against the crotch of her pants. "You want it, don't you?" He unzipped her pants and easily pulled down the loose fitting garment to find a pair of pale green lace panties.

"Damn, you look so delicious. I just can't wait to taste you."

Zara held her breath as Peter dove into her crotch. His lips clasped over her sex and his tongue swept between the moist folds of skin to find the inner core of her most private being.

"Want me to stop?" he said.

Gripping the edge of the desk, she kicked off the pants that still clung to her ankles and brought her legs up into the air.

"That's what I thought," Peter said as he ate her up.

"Here's a little preview of what's to come," he said as he shoved two fingers inside her and moved them in unison to the movements of his mouth on her clitoris.

The double assault was more than she could stand. "Oh, my God."

"Can you imagine my cock in there? It's so hard and big and ready for you. Damn, how I want to fuck you, Zara."

She gasped and threw her head back. "Oh, my God." Her legs straightened out and her toes curled.

"Let me hear you, Zara. I want to hear your sighs, your groans, your gasps."

"Oh!" Her entire body shuddered as he brought her to that beautiful precipice and hung on that all too brief moment before the intense orgasm swept over her.

"I want to be inside you," Peter said as he pulled out his member and stroked it.

"Peter," she protested.

"I know," he groaned as he continued to stroke his engorged cock. "I know."

Zara wrapped her legs around him as he continued stroking.

"Oh, baby. Oh, Zara." He leaned over her just before he climaxed. Breathless, he looked at her and grinned. "I guess this will have to do for now, but just you wait. When we finally make love, when you finally succumb and agree to share a proper bed with me, you'll wonder why you waited so long. Baby, it's going to be so good."

He reached for a handkerchief and wiped her off. "Sorry about the mess."

She grinned as she watched the careful attention he brought to his movements. He was gentle and so caring.

"You're a good man," she said as she ran her fingers through his hair.

"Are you just finding that out?" He tossed the handkerchief into the wastepaper basket and pulled her upright. "I'm a very good man, Zara, and a very good lover." He kissed her, but it was a tender and loving kiss, an after sex kiss that spoke more of heartfelt emotions than passion.

But am I a good enough woman for you? she wondered. She'd never been good at love, and wasn't sure she was capable of loving a man like Peter. He was so handsome, so debonair and so smart. He came from a good family with aristocratic blood, yet he was more humble and hardworking than most men she knew. And she knew he'd love her and treat her like a princess if she so desired.

Then why weren't the emotions there?

"Let's get away for the weekend," he said. "Let's finally make that connection, Zara. Let me show you just how good we can be."

UNASSUMED

"It sounds wonderful, really, but..." She shook her head and dropped her legs from around him. "As enticing as that might be, we've got too much work to do to go away. There was just an attempt on Leo's life, remember?"

He groaned and stepped back, fixing his pants, and adjusting his shirt and tie. "The man acted alone."

"How do you know?" She hopped back into her pants and zipped them up.

"I checked up on him. Turns out he's an orphan, just like you."

Zara stared at him, angry he'd waited so long before sharing such information.

"He was raised in an orphanage."

"What happened to his parents?"

"They had an accident. Can you guess where?"

"Da Hwa," Zara said in a flat tone.

Peter nodded. "His father fell off the roof after trying to repair a leak and his mother died in a fire."

Dreading the rest of the story, Zara buckled her belt and turned to stare out the window.

"Her shirt got caught in the conveyor belt and she was dragged towards the heating elements."

Tears filled her eyes as she envisioned the horror. "So this man, this orphaned child... he blamed Da Hwa?"

"And Leo, as heir to his father's wealth, was the only available target."

"You're sure no one put him up to it."

"Certain."

Wanting to believe Leo was out of danger, Zara nodded. It would explain why the lone gun man had had a gun different from every other member of the crime ring that had been apprehended.

"Leo's safe?" she ventured.

"The word is out; Leo is well surrounded and protection is high. Any would-be kidnappers would be fool to try anything when we're all on such high alert."

Zara couldn't hide her skepticism.

"In addition to that, Leo's reputation as a capable fighter is going around. I think I also heard about a tough, even sexy, badass detective who's on his case."

She hid a shy smile.

"You know, any guy who is protected by you can't help but get a hard on every time you walk into the room."

Her smile widened. Though she tried to be as professional as possible, she knew how men viewed her. "So, what you're saying is that I'm still the best person to protect Leo."

Giving her a playful pat on the butt, he smirked and nodded. "I guess."

"I promise I'll be more careful. I won't allow myself to be blinded by my ultimate goal."

"That's good to hear."

She quietly looked at him. "I think we also need to address your feelings for me, Peter. The distraction could be enough to get us into danger as well."

"Okay, I see your point."

"Which brings us back to the possibility of transferring."

"Be honest, Zara. Would you like to see me transfer for our mutual safety, or is it because of Leo?"

"Peter, you know I care about you. You know I have feelings for you, even if I'm a little confused by everything at the moment."

He pulled her in for a breathtaking kiss. "I know. I've always known."

"We both need to be more vigilant and not let our emotions get in the way. I wouldn't want anything to happen to you either." She set a light kiss on his nose.

"Sometimes I really don't care what happens to me. I'm just worried about you."

"Well then, think about what would become of me if ever something were to happen to you."

"Okay."

"I love working with you, but... I think a transfer would be best... for both of us."

"Okay, how 'bout this? The moment we get a good head on this case, I'll back off. It shouldn't be much longer now."

"We just need to take a close look at the people around Leo's father."

"And if you can remember any details about that old man who wanted you to work for him, it would be the breakthrough we need."

Chapter 17

Zara

Zara returned to the hospital to talk to Leo hoping to get a few answers about the orphaned gun man, but when that proved fruitless, she headed to the clinic in Kowloon to talk to her grandmother.

"I'm sorry I wasn't here when you woke up, Nana."

The old woman patted Zara's hand. "I know you're very busy. Don't worry about your old Nana. She'll do fine."

"I hate to question you while you're still recovering, but…"

"Ask, ask, my dear Zara."

"I always thought the martial arts I was taught as a child were… well, exclusive. Was that just my childish memory of my lessons with Uncle Chang?"

"Chang brought many elements from many arts together. It made for a very original fighting tool. No one else teach like he teach."

"That's what I thought, but... I had to fight a man off recently, and I was surprised to see how he matched me move for move... certain moves that I distinctly remember learning from Chang who'd claimed to have invented them."

The old hooded eyes widened in surprise, but she had no answer to offer Zara.

"Does the name Fong ring a bell?"

Again, no useful answer.

"Nana, the man I fought with, his name was Fong, and his parents lived in the same village as Mom and Dad."

Nana looked up at her with sadness in her eyes, but said nothing.

"What really happened to them, Nana?"

"An accident."

"What kind of accident?"

"Run off the road... into a ditch."

"I always thought they simple jobs, but... They had other jobs, didn't they?"

"Your father was a food inspector. He traveled from town to town inspecting various factories for cleanliness, food temperatures and adequate safety and equipment standards... things like that."

Zara immediately made the connection with Da Hwa. Surely her father had visited the old building a few times.

Nana hesitated. "Your mother was a teacher."

"Okay." That seemed simple enough.

"At the elementary school in the village."

She said it with such purpose, Zara's ears perked up.

"All children from the village attended that school. Your mother taught many children."

"You mean this Fong was taught by Mom?"

"She once mentioned a young boy who'd lost his father and was so distraught. He withdrew into himself and hardly spoke to anyone."

"I never knew that."

"Your mother felt certain she could draw him out of his gloom by introducing him to Sifu Master Chang."

Zara gasped. She'd almost been killed by a man her mother had tried to save from himself. But all this didn't explain why this man tried to kill Leo. He'd been orphaned for so long, what could have set him off so suddenly?

Or better yet, who had tipped him off, perhaps even goading him into going after Leo?

Chapter 18

Zara

Zara sat in the private jet with Peter, heading out for her surprise weekend with Peter in London. Sitting in his family's private jet was so romantic, almost a fairy tale.

"Aren't you glad you finally decided to come?" he'd said the moment they'd arrived at the country estate, which looked like a scene out of a Jane Austen novel.

It was magnificent, and Zara could easily imagine moving her life to such a lovely setting. But the biggest surprise had come that Saturday night. After a sumptuous dinner accompanied by two exquisite bottles of wine, Peter had led her to his large airy bedroom.

"We have the entire place to ourselves tonight. My parents will be arriving tomorrow evening for dinner, which I promise won't be like those dreadful British dinners you watch on film. My father is a bit stodgy like fathers tend to be, who are respectable and authoritative; but my mother…you remind me of a lot like her. Strong backbone and all."

"I know. We met briefly when I was here last time. For the holidays?"

"Oh, I'm sorry, I nearly forgot you met them before. It was a while back, though, and I just wanted to jog your memory of them. This weekend, I want it to be absolutely perfect for you. For us." He kissed her and began undressing her. I don't think I can wait any longer," he said as he guided her to the bed, laying her there.

Her head soaked with red wine and her body hungering for release from a stressful week, she didn't argue or resist. Her body wanted him, wanted the pleasure it could bring her, and to continue what started at Peter's office between them. It was heavenly, and she wanted more of what he promised.

He peeled back the soft, diaphanous panels of her summer dress, exposing the body she worked hard to keep toned and fit. "You're so beautiful, Zara," Peter said. With tender loving kisses, he explored every inch of her sexy body. By the time he brought his lips back to hers, she could barely stand it.

UNASSUMED

Zara didn't want to think about Leo. She didn't want to think there was a slight possibility with him. She would only be a notch on his bedpost, another plaything that he bedded, like Vanessa See, who was obviously having sex with him at the hotel room. Although Leo's touch always brought up a strong reaction to him, Zara couldn't dare think about anything further. Not anymore. He was her charge, nothing more. She needed to get him out of her head so she could do her job without getting tangled in jealousy over seeing some naked woman emerge from his hotel room. "Make love to me," she demanded Peter. "I want you all over me, Peter. Make me yours."

"I'm going to fuck you, to make love to you, to pleasure you, anything and everything you want," he said hoarsely yet softly.

And he didn't disappoint her. His movements were like warm liquid honey, drizzling over her body and making her feel better than she could have ever imagined. He was careful and loving when he drove himself deep inside her hot and wet core, but the loving pace quickly gave way to such a powerful and passionate pounding as Peter acted out his pent up desires for her, Zara was left breathless as they both climaxed together, with Peter sliding his fingers through the fingers of both her hands while pushing far and deep into her.

"Didn't I tell you?" he said breathlessly. "How good we'd be together? Don't you regret having put this off for so long?"

"You are wonderful, Peter," Zara smiled into his eyes. "I didn't know it would be this good, and I do love it here... with you. It's magical. You make me feel like a princess."

"This could be your life, Zara ... every day." He nuzzled into her neck. "Every night." He rolled off the bed, opened the top drawer of the bedside table and dropped to his knees.

"Peter? What are you doing?"

The little blue box in his hand was all the answer she needed. Her heart pounded as he offered it to her, his eyes wide with love, and a hint of fear.

"This can't be a surprise to you, Zara. You know how I feel about you."

"Yes, but..."

"I don't expect you to answer me tonight. Think it over, consider how you feel here, at the estate, in England. This is what I have to offer you."

"Peter," Zara said, surprised, "I…I have to talk to Nana. After all, she's all I have, and she just had surgery. I have to consider her. I want to say 'yes', but I have to think it over."

"I know, Zara," Peter said. "That's why I don't expect an answer from you yet. I know how important your grandmother is to you so please ask for her advice. In the meantime," Peter smiled. "How about round two?" He kissed her and began teasing her warm heated flesh below with his fingers, making her close her eyes and moan while biting her lower lips. "You look so hot when you're enjoying my touch…"

They continued making love and exploring each other all night, and woke up to voices in the foyer the next morning.

Peter's parents had arrived early.

"Hello? Peter?" Lady Brock knocked on the door, causing Peter and Zara to hastily scramble into their clothes.

"What is it, Mother?" Peter called out.

"Just letting you know your father and I are here early. I can't wait to see you, my darling boy! We've missed you, with you being in Hong Kong and all. Extending your trip there another year instead of returning home. Have you finally proposed to that girl? You know, the girl who is the reason why you're in Hong Kong all this time?"

Peter looked at Zara and shrugged sheepishly. "Mother just wants to be a grandmother soon, that's all," he smiled to Zara. "Stay here, and I'll go out to greet my parents. You can get ready for breakfast with them out on the terrace facing the gardens. Just something simple. A summer dress would do. I'll have a word with them to let them know you're here, too. Staying with me in my room."

Zara blushed. "Should I get another room? Should we even..."

"Zara, I'm in my late twenties. I'm nearly thirty years old. My parents would have to realize I'm an adult with adult urges, and since I'm here with my special woman, I expect to be spending some time with her here, too." He smiled. "They love you already, Zara. Since the holidays. Mother has been pressuring me to finally ask you to marry me."

Zara smiled widely. "You mean they've accepted me?"

"How could they not?" Peter said, pulling her into his chest and hugging her. "You make me happy.

UNASSUMED

You turned me into a responsible and hard-working grown man instead of a spoiled British playboy, which would have been my path have I not caught sight of you on my trip to Hong Kong with my father years ago. You helped me fall into a career I have a passion and devotion to thanks to you. And, my dear Zara," he kissed her on top of her head. "You made me into a man my parents could respect and be proud of."

"Peter, I did not! You did that all on your own, and…"

"It wouldn't be possible if I hadn't fallen for you and followed you into law enforcement. I was just going to sit back and help run my father's business from some tower, but with you, I can't let anyone else be near you, watch over you, for fear they would snatch you away, Zara."

"Peter, you care that much for me?"

"Since you don't believe me when I say 'I love you', I've been showing you that I do in these ways."

"Oh Peter," Zara said, hugging him tightly. "I don't deserve you. You are too good for me. I…"

"Just say 'yes' to me, Zara." Peter held her. "It would make me the happiest man alive."

"Peter?" Peter's mom was knocking at the door again. "Are you even in there? Maybe not since no one is responding. I'm coming in…"

Peter quickly shoved Zara away from the door when it opened, and a tall elegant older woman in her fifties with fading auburn hair in a chin-length bob walked through. She was dressed in a Chanel yellow suit, and looked very much like her title, Lady Penelope Brock.

"Hi Mother," Peter kissed her on both cheeks. "You're looking radiant."

"And so do you, Peter," she said looking at him and his glowing face. She looked around his room, and walked up straight to the heavy curtains, pulling it open. "You need more fresh air, though. It smells musky in here, and…oh hi…Zara?"

Zara walked out of the bathroom in a sunny yellow lace sundress and white high heel sandals. Her hair was pinned back with a pretty dairy and diamond hair clip, and she wore a bright coral lipstick that brighten her entire face. "Hi Lady Brock," she said, walking up to her and giving her a hug. "I hope your trip here was nice."

"Oh, Zara, aren't you adorable?" Lady Brock smiled widely. "And I almost forgot how pretty you are…no wonder my Peter is all heads over heels for you."

Zara looked over at Peter and caught his quick smile. He was also nodding his approval of her prim but proper and very sweet look.

"Lady Brock, you look radiant. Your trip to Spain must've have been exciting. You must tell me all about it."

"Oh, I wish you and Peter were on the cruise with us. It would've been so much fun with you two around instead of me with old hubs," Lady Brock said. "Next time, I would love for you two to come along. I want us to have more family trips together, especially when the little ones come along. I want to be able to see them all the time, and you can drop them off with me while I care for them on weekends…"

Zara couldn't help liking this vivacious woman next to her.

Peter came up behind her while she walked with Lady Brock. "You could call her 'mom' too," he said smiling.

Zara nearly elbowed him. "Subtle, Peter…"

"I want you to picture life with me, Zara. Family trips..."

"I love what you did with the wallpaper in the dining room, Lady Brock," Zara said to her hostess.

"You do? I thought it was time to let go of the stodgy velvet paisley print and bring in some pastel swirls and florals."

"It modernizes the entire room," Zara said.

"I'm glad someone here appreciates the efforts I've made to bring this old estate into the new century," Lady Brock said.

"And you can help Mother out some more when we come out here to visit," Peter said.

"That would be so nice," Lady Brock said. "I would love the company. We have so much land here and the place is so large. There are only the two of us here, me and the old man, with Peter off in Hong Kong and all. I would love to see this place filled with children and parties, and..."

"Well, there you are," a large man with grey hair and grey eyes wearing a black suit walked into the foyer where they were. "Peter, you brought your girl," he smiled at Zara and looked her up and down appreciatively. "Just like you've described her, too."

241

"Hi Zara," he bent down to kiss one of her cheeks, "Happy to have you here. Welcome back to Brockshire."

"Thank you, Lord Brock," Zara said smiling and feeling a little uneasy and awkward around the great bear of a man who stood next to Peter and Penelope Brock. He wasn't as accepting of her as Peter's mother, and Zara could sense a strange coldness in his eyes toward her.

"Well, let's go have breakfast on the terrace this morning." He turned to Peter. "I'm sorry, son, but I have to cut this weekend short. I have to fly out to Macao this evening for a meeting so we'll have this brunch instead of dinner."

"Fine, Dad," Peter said. "As long as you can have it with all of us, including Zara, that's fine."

"Great, so now, Zara…" Lord Brock eyed her while the maids poured coffee and tea into each of their cups. "What important cases have you been working on?"

"Dad?" Peter said, embarrassed. "No talk about cases here. We're not allowed to discuss any of the details outside, and you can't get anything out of Zara, too."

"Just wanted to see how dedicated your potential fiancé is to her work before she decides to chuck it to come live out here with you and Mom."

Peter shifted uncomfortably in his chair. "I know how dedicated Zara is to her work, but she has a life of her own outside of work, as do I, and we want to make the most of it here or anywhere we decide to live after we get married."

Zara shifted uncomfortably in her chair now.

"Peter," Lady Brock exclaimed excitedly, "did she say 'yes'?" She turned to Zara, "You did say 'yes' to Peter's proposal, didn't you? Please tell me you did. I would die if you didn't agree to marry Peter, after all these years he had been waiting for you, been in love with you. It would break his heart and mine if…"

"Mother!" Peter said, reaching for Zara's hand.

Lady Brock looked dismayed and upset. "Peter, I just wanted Zara to know how you felt. You've never been able to get your feelings across well since you were a little boy. You always put others' feelings above your own first before letting yours known and, well, here I wanted you to at least tell Zara…"

"Mother, Zara knows exactly how I feel about her. We spent the night in my bed together. Together," he said, with emphasis, looking pointedly at his mother.

"Oh," Lady Brock said. "I…"

"It's okay," Zara said, putting down the toast she was buttering. "I know how much Peter's happiness means to you and you love your son very much, which I can understand. He's a wonderful man. And I would be a fool not to have any feelings for him, too."

"Please tell me you said, 'yes'," Lady Brock said.

Zara looked to Peter and then to Lady Brock's desperate face. "I…"

"Mother!" Peter said, "Zara said…"

"Yes," Zara said. "I told him I will ask my grandmother first. Peter proposed last night in bed, and well, my head's spinning, but I realize how much I care for him, and it's 'yes'."

Lady Brock's eyes widen and her mouth opened into a big wide smile. "Yes?"

Peter was the most surprised one of the bunch. He got up and pulled Zara up with him. "Yes? You said 'yes'?" He let out a big whoop and swept her up into his arms and kissed her hard. "I can't believe it. I

244

can't believe it. I am in shock. I am the most happiest shocked man in the world right now."

"Well, congratulations!" Lord Brock said, slapping his son's back. "I knew this girl's going to make a man of you."

He bent and kissed Zara on top of her head. "Welcome to the family."

The rest of the breakfast or brunch as it turned out to be was a fog for Zara. She sat through conversations between Peter and his parents about arrangements for a wedding. Of course Lady Brock wanted to hold the wedding at Brockshire. Peter wanted to, too, but also wanted to hold a reception back in Hong Kong, where he intended to live with Zara in a high rise. He will be taking over his father's job in a few years, and having Zara, a girl from Hong Kong, whom the citizens admire as one of their own, especially a police officer who had help their communities, would seal the deal for his job as the trade commissioner between Hong Kong and England.

When Peter and Zara finished up with brunch and headed back to their room, Zara was feeling exhausted. She had agreed to marry Peter before she talked to her grandmother. Why did she acted so hastily?

"Having second thoughts about saying 'yes' to me?" Peter asked, walking up to her from behind and wrapping his arms around her waist before nuzzling her neck. "If you do, I will work on erasing any and all doubts right now." He began unzipping her dress, and letting it fall to the ground, while one hand dipped inside her lace panties to find the moist and heated folds of skin he was seeking.

"Ohhh, Peter," Zara leaned back against his chest.

He increased his pressure on her folds, dipping his fingers inside. "You looked so cute and sexy all dolled up in this dress this morning, Zara. I wanted to tear it off and lay you down on top of the table and fuck you right there. But..."

"But parents were there," Zara laughed.

"But not right here," Peter said, turning her around and removing her bra. He dipped his head down and placed his mouth on top of her breast and sucked hard while licking her nipples, flicking each until they were hard as pebbles.

"Peter..."

"Zara, last night was not enough. I need to have you right now."

He continued his tongue's assault on her breast but lifted her and carried her to the bed where he slowly made love to her, bringing her to orgasm.

They continued making love and trying all kinds of positions in bed and out of bed all morning and then into the afternoon, until it was dark.

After their ninth or tenth orgasm, Zara climbed out of bed and said, "Peter! Your parents. Are they still here? Did they leave? Oh no, we have to say bye to them."

Zara turned to Peter, and she had to laugh. He was knocked out, exhausted from all their physical activities. She got out of bed, took a shower, and got dressed. She had to go out to say something to her new future in-laws before they took off and don't see each other for months.

The house was dark, but there was a light coming from the end of the hallway from Peter's parents' room. She was going to go knock on their door when she heard a voice talking, angrily.

She followed the voice and was about to walk into what looked like a library, but saw that the door was nearly shut, and someone had their back to the door. It was Lord Brock, and he was on the phone.

Oh, thank heavens, Lord Brock was still here. That means she could say her good-byes, and maybe get to know her future father-in-law better.

But the tone of his voice clearly stated that he was in the middle of a heated conversation. No doubt business-related. She would have to wait for the conversation to be over, but she didn't want to miss him on his way out.

"What do you mean the deal in Hong Kong didn't go through? I thought you greased the hands of that inspector pretty well or are you telling me these chumps want more? Keep an eye on him, and if he thinks he can bypass my authority, we'll have to send him a message. Yeah, the same way as always. Now how's Macao? I shouldn't have to fly in tonight if you ran things more smoothly. Yeah, I have to interrupt an important family occasion to fly in to get the job done. If you show any more of that incompetency, I wouldn't have a need for you any longer, you know what I mean…Good so you understand. Ship up or the next time you hear from me, it will be the last."

Zara didn't want to be hearing this conversation but she thought something was suspicious. She knew she should talk to Peter about it first, but something about the way Peter and his father interacted showed Peter barely knew what his father did as a commissioner. She was about to head back to Peter's room when Lord Brock startled her by walking out of the library, his face red with anger.

"Oh, hi," Zara said. "I was just coming down to see if you and Lady Brock would be able to stay for the evening. Peter and I wanted to get some dinner in town, but if you are staying, we can have dinner here…"

Lord Brock's mind was preoccupied, but he looked up and watched Zara's face. It was a dimly-lit room, and she was standing in the hallway, which made her even hard to see.

"You just came by just now?" he asked.

"Yes," she said. "I saw you were busy so I stepped away but came back just now."

"How much did you hear of my conversation?" he asked, his eyes narrowing.

"Conversation?" she asked. "I barely noticed you were on the phone. I just heard your voice, but thought you were busy so I went away. Didn't hear anything at all. Nothing but the sound of your voice. I couldn't even tell you if you were speaking English or Cantonese or whatever..."

He looked hard at her and then nodded. "It's a good thing Peter is crazy about you. At first I wondered what kind of girl would make my son lose his head and drop everything just to remain in Hong Kong after his first trip, and it seems the type of girl happens to be a smart one – one who knows how to mind her business, one who knows how to stay quiet when she needs it, and one who knows not to question certain things the elders have worked hard on for years to put in place."

Zara remained expressionless, but nodded. "Peter seems to know what he wants."

"He is a good boy, and he has a kind heart," Lord Brock said. "But he also knows what to do when he wants to get what he wants. He's a go-getter, Zara. He got you, didn't he?"

Zara almost choke when he said that, but then she felt a hand on her shoulder and turned around. "Zara, so there you are," Peter said. "I was looking for you, and I thought I heard voices." He looked over at his father. "So Dad, are you staying for dinner or do you still have plans to fly to Macao?"

Lord Brock looked at Zara. "I'm afraid I have to fly to Macao. My men there can't seem to handle the slightest problems. I can't wait to retire, but then again, I will only retire when Peter can handle my job. Right, Peter?"

Peter beamed. "If I get appointed in, Dad. Those are big shoes to fill. And it's very political. I don't know if I have the finesse..."

"You do and you will," Lord Brock said. "You've already got this lovely girl from Hong Kong to agree to marry you. And you hold a very respectable job in Hong Kong. You will have the respect and confidence of people from Hong Kong and here behind you."

"Thank you, Dad, for the vote of confidence," Peter beamed. "I will try my best."

"Good, good!" Lord Brock said. "Now where is Penelope? I promised her an unforgettable dinner in Macao if she can come with me tonight." He leaned into Peter and nudged him with his shoulder, "That would leave you two alone for the rest of the evening. I see how you two are. Disappearing into your room for hours. I know you two rather spend the evening together alone than with us old folks getting in the way."

Zara blushed while Peter laughed.

"Go on now, kids," Lord Brock said. "I'll get Penelope, and we'll say our good-byes and get out of your hair right afterwards. I can see how Peter is eager to get back to whatever it was you two were doing before we came out here."

"Dad!" Peter said. "Zara and I have a lot of planning to do, and…"

"Yeah, so that's what you call it nowadays…back in our day…"

"Dad!"

Penelope came over and said, "There you all are…it's like a maze here sometimes. I have to tie a string to your Dad to be able to find him in this house. It's enormous. Well. I did hear him saying how we have to get going to Macao. It's late, and we will leave you two alone. The faster I can think of having little ones running around this place on holidays," she squealed. "I can't wait to become a grandma! Oh, Zara, I just love you. You made me so very happy."

Zara couldn't help smiling back. "You too, Lady Brock."

Penelope took Lord Brock's hand and said, "We have to get going now. I want them to get started on their honeymoon..."

"Mother, not you too?" Peter looked at Zara and whispered, "See, sharing a room together wasn't all that bad. It's expected."

Zara blushed while the Brocks looked at her with smiles on their faces.

When Lord and Lady Brock left, Peter swept her into his arms and said, "Now, where were we, my beautiful fiancé?" He kissed her and said, "I still can't believe you're finally mine. I don't know how I can stand not being able to touch you all the time when we're together at the office..." He smiled. "We can have a short engagement period and then the wedding, but knowing my mother, she would want a big society wedding."

Zara smiled but looked down. She already loved being part of Peter's family, but something was nagging at her, and it had something to do with Lord Brock's conversation. It was a side of him she didn't expect to find, and the thinly veiled threat he planted on her when he bumped into her in the hallway made her uneasy. What exactly was Lord Brock's work in Macao and Hong Kong, and would she want Peter to follow in those footsteps once they were married?

Zara and Peter went out to a pub for dinner and a beer and a game of darts after Lord and Lady Brock left. It was a pleasant diversion from their everyday life in Hong Kong, and Peter bumped into a few classmates while there.

They were excited for Peter after hearing his engagement with Zara, and said he couldn't do better, knowing how he could barely ask a girl out back when he was in school. Peter laughed it off, and seemed to fit right in with everyone as though he had never left for Hong Kong.

After returning back to their room, Peter surprised Zara with red roses on the bed and in the hot tub. He had champagne on ice and even chocolate strawberries. "I thought we'd have dessert and a bath before bed," he said. "What do you think?"

"Peter," Zara said, "You're so amazing. This is wonderful, and…"

"Zara, if you had said, 'no', I probably would have kept trying. This is Plan B, and I had a Plan C and a D..."

"Peter, your father was right," Zara said.

"About what?" he asked, cocking his head.

"About you knowing how to get what you want."

"Did I get what I wanted?" Peter asked.

"I'm here, aren't I?" Zara said. "And we had sex for the first time together and many times afterwards, and..."

"Okay," Peter said, "You got me. I did get what I wanted. I wanted to bed you and to devour you, and..." He laughed. "I got more than I wished, today Zara. But of course I want more, and soon, we will have all that."

*****

The flight back was as romantic as the entire weekend. Peter held Zara in his arms the entire way and kept kissing her. He kept telling her how he could die a happy man knowing she loved him and wanted to marry him. The weekend felt so magical to Zara, she didn't want to see it end so when Peter told her he thought about it a lot through the trip, that he wanted her to move in with him; she hesitated and said she'll have to think about it. Seeing her grandmother brought back her reality, and it was something she had to bring up with Peter. What was she going to do with Grandma being in Hong Kong?

Also, there was the whole incidence with Lord Brock. Something was up, and her detective instincts told her it wasn't as unassuming as it seemed. She had to check him out.

Back at work the following Monday, Zara felt the entire fairy tale and fantasy fall apart in front of her as she stared into some hidden files on the screen.

Lord Brock had his hands in almost every transaction between Hong Kong and England and then Macao where there was some police activity, which then got cleared immediately.

She looked for the reason why they were cleared, and saw that it was due to mislabeling of products. What was thought of as illegal, was actually mislabeled in the first place, but the products coming through were cleared.

Years ago, there were several shipments between Da Hwa and England, as well as France. Again, there was an inspection that blocked some shipments until Lord Brock signed them through.

The following day, when she went into Lee Holdings, she was able to pull up Da Hwa's shipment information and see that Lord Brock had waived some inspections of shipments. She looked at the shipment logistics of one particular shipment to England, France, and other parts from Da Hwa and noticed that was the time Da Hwa began losing sales. Yet the shipments were consistent with previous years.

"Leo," Zara said. "Can we find anyone who worked at the factory at the time these shipments were made?"

"I can get my guys to look up old employee records and see where they moved," Leo said.

"Good," Zara said smiling at Leo, "I think I'm onto something with Da Hwa that could lead to us finding out why it was closed down, and why that man wanted to kill you. Maybe it will lead to finding out who is behind the crime ring?"

"Sure," Leo said, watching her closely. He was acting friendly enough with her, but the tension between them before had dissipated a bit since she got back from England, and showed him her ring.

He was silent and distant after that, and Zara knew it was because she was officially off the market for him, and he wanted to respect that. It was an odd feeling, but Zara felt strange showing him the ring at first, but she felt like she had to in order to set things straight between them once and for all. It also gave Peter his sense of control back.

Accepting Peter's proposal was the right thing for her to do. She knew that now.

But then again, she was becoming more and more unsure about Lord Brock.

Chapter 19

Zara

Zara had a break through the next day when Leo called her into his office.

"Guess what?" he said excitedly. "We found a woman who worked at the factory stuffing the packets into the noodle packages right here in town. She lives with her daughter down the street. I've arranged for you to meet her for coffee near her apartment."

"When?"

"She's at Heavenly Café just down the street, go now, and you should be able to catch her. She goes by Mrs. Yip."

"Great, thanks, Leo, this is going to hopefully help our case."

"Good, anything to help," he said looking unusually cheerful.

Zara ran out to the elevators and out to the street to Heavenly Café just in time to see a woman in her fifties wearing a jogging suit walk out of the café. "Mrs. Yip?" Zara asked.

UNASSUMED

The woman looked cautiously at Zara and then saw that she had a badge from Lee Holdings. "Yes, Zara Zee?"

"Yes, please don't go yet, I need to ask a few questions."

"What can I help you with?"

"When you worked at Da Hwa, did you get a chance to see what were in those flavor packets? Did you get a chance to see what was in any of the packages that was sent to England and Europe?"

"Oh those? They were specially marked shipments. We made the noodles the same way as everyone else's but the flavorings had to be changed to suit their taste. We didn't have the ingredients for those specially marked flavors in the factory, so they came from elsewhere. Some were pre-packaged. All we did was stuffed them in with the noodle packages."

"Did you see where those special flavor packages were from?"

"I couldn't tell. They weren't labeled, and were brought in through special carriers. Must've been some kind of super fancy flavor," she laughed.

"Anything you can remember about the delivery trucks? The uniforms of these men?"

"Come to think of it, the delivery trucks had the word, 'Glorias Flavor' on there."

"Okay, that is very helpful," Zara said. "Can I get you anything? More coffee? Cake?"

"Just knowing someone cared about what happened at Da Hwa is payment enough," Mrs. Yip said. "I loved working there, and met my husband through the factory. We have a daughter together, and it wouldn't be possible if we had never been working there."

"Thank you, Mrs. Yip, I will let the Chairman of Lee Holdings know. He would appreciate hearing that the factory did have some good to it."

"My pleasure," Mrs. Yip said and left.

Zara walked back to the office and pulled up more records of suppliers to Da Hwa and saw that Glorias Flavor was some dubious company that had been cited and busted for being part of a drug trafficking ring, back at the time Da Hwa was using them.

Oh no, Zara thought. Please don't let it be what I think it is.

Then she pulled up more records of Glorias Flavor supplying other goods to other factories which were shipped to England and Europe. All signed for by Lord Brock.

That night she had to tell Peter what she had decided on whether to move in with him so they met for dinner.

"Feeling better about being back in Hong Kong?" Peter said.

"Hardly," she lied. "I can't stop thinking about that estate. It's the type of place you read about, the type of place you dream of visiting."

"Imagine living there."

"I'll admit, it's very enticing."

"I'm happy to hear that."

"You know, if we do move to England and you take on your father's role as commissioner, and I manage to get a position that pays moderately well, we might have a hard time with the upkeep of such a large estate, don't you think?"

"Hmmm, you make a good point. I know my father has struggled to maintain the place in tip top shape from time to time, but he's managed. I guess I will too."

"How much do you estimate it will cost to keep it running so smoothly?"

He shrugged. "Oh, I don't know. I would imagine a few hundred thousand dollars should cover it… a million tops."

"Our combined salaries couldn't possibly cover that."

"Well then, we'd just have to find a way to make it work… cut back on the staff. We'll see when the time comes."

"But how does your father manage? It must be impossible."

A vague look came over Peter's handsome face. "Look, I'll admit I've asked myself that question a few times. A man in my father's position is easy to bribe. There are lots of people all over the world who could benefit from a favor from my father."

"I hate to say this, Peter, but I think we're going to have to take a closer look at your father."

His face blank, he nodded. Then he let out a big sigh, "He's my father, but I'm going to do what's right, Zara. What do you have on him?"

Zara pulled out a few folders and said, "He had been accepting bribes for years, mainly from factories who were aiding drug traffickers to push heroin into Europe – England, France, Italy…"

"Oh my God," Peter said, wiping his brow. "How did you find out?"

"Looking at records, interviewing a woman who worked there...finding out what Glorias Flavor was."

"I can't believe it," Peter said. "I don't want to believe it, but I have to question him on it, and I don't know what it will all mean?"

"I'm sorry to be the bearer of bad news on this, Peter," Zara said, "But he may have something to do with some of the inspections at Da Hwa too."

"Your parents?" Peter looked angry. "Are you telling me my father may have something to do with your parents' deaths?"

"No, no," Zara said. "I think he deals with shady characters and..."

"I won't be like him when I become Commissioner, Zara," Peter said.

"Peter, I'm sorry about your father."

"Me, too, Zara, but just because he's my father doesn't mean I have to shirk my duties in investigating him for being part of the organized crime ring. Like I said, I will do what I have to."

264

"This…your father knows I knew something was up," Zara said.

"I love you Zara, and even if I don't get my father's approval in marrying you, it doesn't affect how I feel about you or that I still intend on marrying you." Peter sighed. "I'm sorry, Zara, but I need some time alone to myself tonight. I have to process this, and it's just a bit much right now."

Chapter 20

Zara

Disheartened, Zara sat back in the old vinyl chair in her cramped little office the following morning. His father's influence reached to virtually every corner of the world.

"Peter," she said as she rang his office. "Could you come see me?"

"Be right there."

She knew it was going to be difficult, but it had to be done. Sullen, Peter walked in and took the chair facing her and sat down. "What do you have?"

"More details you should know. First of all, Leo was mistaken. Harold wasn't involved in any of this, but Tommy Leung was in it up to his elbows."

Peter flipped through the profile on Tommy. "Head of operation and supervisor at Da Hwa for over eight years."

"Exactly."

"But it says here he lost his leg in an accident and had to leave Da Hwa."

"Right again. He took an early retirement, but he made regular visits to his *buddies* at the factory."

"Oh?"

"He ran a very lucrative heroin smuggling operation via those flavor packets in the noodle packages."

"Smart, I guess."

"The boxes were specially marked and... well, your father simply let them slip in without going through customs."

Peter went white.

"I'm sorry, Peter."

"Go on."

"As time went on, Tommy became more and more confident, and perhaps a little less vigilant. An inspector made a surprise visit one day and became suspicious. He forced one of the workers to open one of the specially marked boxes and found the heroine. That afternoon, he was run off the road."

"Do we know who that inspector was?"

Zara swallowed the pain and heartache that seemed so insurmountable. "His name was Hulin Zee."

Frowning, Peter looked up at her. "Zee?"

She nodded. "My father was that inspector."

Ashamed and guilt-ridden, Peter set his face in his hands in disgrace. "Oh, my God."

"So Leo's father was running a decent operation."

"All on the up and up."

"But his employees took advantage of his trust."

"There's some indication in here that he was beginning to suspect something was going on. Maybe all the lost profits, or the number of missing shipments, but... well, he never had the chance to investigate further. He grew ill and his health became his priority."

"What happened when he died and Leo took over?"

"They tried to figure out just what Leo knew, but he'd been away in the States when a lot of this happened, and once he returned to Hong Kong he was caught up with the opening of his restaurant the Oyster House. All those preoccupations probably saved his life. If he'd taken too much interest in the goings on at Lee Holdings, he probably would have been snuffed out more expediently."

268

"As it was, they had free reign."

"More or less. They had to move their operation to another factory, but aside from that, it was business as usual. "

"Man, what an operation."

"They even made sure Leo was kept busy, day and night, with parties, pretty women and a large variety of toys… cars, motorbikes, planes."

"Then why these recent attempts?"

"Apparently Leo had started to ask a few questions, and they got nervous, so they implemented an insider."

"You got a name?"

"Qingshan," Zara said. "Qingshan Lee."

Peter stared at her in disbelief.

"Leo's trusted advisor?"

"And favorite uncle." She shook her head in dismay. "We knew this ring liked to get in close, but never thought they would get in this close."

"I think we owe Qingshan a little visit."

Zara stood and reached for her gun belt. "I'm right behind you."

They arrived at Lee Holdings and Zara made the familiar journey to the administrative floor, but instead of heading to the right to find Leo's office, she turned to the left and came to Qingshan's office.

"Hello, Uncle Qingshan," Zara said in a cheery, upbeat voice. She'd met him only twice before, and he'd insisted on the familiarity.

"Zara , I thought you were at the hospital with your grandmother. How is she?"

"Recovering. Thank you for asking."

"Well, it's always a pleasure to see you. What brings you to my office?"

"To be honest, I'm a little worried about Leo. He's been really distant lately, and I don't know what to make of it."

"Leo's always been an over achiever. His head is in a dozen projects at the same time; his restaurant, a new movie, a new flame. Who know? Don't take it personally."

Zara smiled shyly. "I'm trying." Her eye caught on a photo of a little boy walking between two sharply dressed men. All three wore super cool sunglasses. "Is that Leo?"

Qingshan nodded.

"That is so adorable."

"Leo's always been my favorite, and even more so since his father died."

"You must really love him to come to Lee Holdings as his advisor," Peter said.

"Leo's never had a head for business."

"And what kind of business background do you have?"

Qingshan frowned and directed a glare at Peter.

"I spent a good portion of the day yesterday going through the books," Peter said. "And there are a few numbers that just don't add up."

"What are you saying exactly?"

"I'm saying that millions of dollars are mysteriously disappearing, not to mention missing shipments, and a few inexplicable accidents."

Qingshan rose and calmly made his way to the small bar where he poured some tea. Setting two cups before his guests, he said, "I have a feeling we're going to have a lot to discuss. I think Leo may have been a little dishonest." He returned to pour himself a cup of tea and returned to his large leather chair.

Raising his cup of tea, he invited his guests to do the same. "Now, let's try to sort this mess out."

UNASSUMED

They sipped their tea, and while Zara found it
unusually bitter, she didn't want to insult Qingshan by
not drinking it, but before she finished her last sip, the
room around her began to spin, and soon, everything
went dull grey and finally pitch black.

Chapter 21

Zara

"Peter?" Zara called out in the dark, cold room.

"Right beside you. I was beginning to wonder if you'd ever wake up."

"Any idea where we are?"

"No, but it smells like hell in here."

"Like a dozen rotting rats."

"I've got a knife in my boot. Can you reach down and get it."

Zara shrugged and struggled and managed to slip out of the hastily knotted rope around her wrists. "No need," she said with a clap of her hands.

"Great. I've been sitting here for over an hour waiting for you to wake up, and you instantly break free. I should have kicked you awake the minute I woke up."

"Sometimes you're just too much of a gentleman." She pulled apart the rope that bound him

273

and quickly turned to the source of light streaming in under a door. "This is our way out."

He came up behind her as she opened the door and checked to make sure they were alone.

"Are we in a barn?"

"Looks like it may once have been."

Dry strands of hay and straw littered the dirt floor and a variety of farm tools stood rusting in a corner. Zara carefully headed to the stalls, inspecting them one after the other.

At the third, she stopped and threw her head back in disgust. "Argh," she said, holding back on a serious gag. "Now I know where that stink of death is coming from."

Peter joined her and looked inside the stall. Blood stained three corners of the stall that was equipped with harnesses and chains.

"This is where they brought them," Peter muttered. "All those kidnap victims."

Zara wanted to throw up as she thought of the heirs who'd been kidnapped and tortured. "I think I see a finger," she said.

Peter entered the stall and carefully picked up the digit in a clean white hanky, wrapped it up and put it in his jacket pocket. "Why would someone go to all this trouble? Just to eliminate competition? Just to make more money? It's so disgusting."

"And to think that Leo's uncle is behind all this," Zara said with disbelief.

Her quiet mourning for the victims she'd been unable to save was interrupted by the loud roar of a vehicle approaching.

"Come on," Peter said as he quickly ushered her back into the room they'd been locked in.

He needn't explain what the plan was. Zara knew him well enough to know how he thought. In silence they waited in the cold, dark room, and as expected, they soon heard footsteps approaching. Zara closed her eyes and concentrated on the sound of the steps to determine how many men they could expect. It sounded like only one. It would be a piece of cake taking him down.

The door eased open and light streamed in. Holding her breath, Zara waited until the man had completely entered the room before charging him. Peter joined in and finished him off with a sound punch in the nose.

"That was easy enough," he said proudly.

Her gut twisted in a knot and she pressed her lips together. It'd been a little too easy.

"Come on," Peter said as he stepped out of the darkened room. "We'll take his car and head back into town." He'd barely taken two steps out when he was jumped by three men.

While two of the men pinned Peter to the ground, the third prepared to pummel him, Zara pounced on the tall man, biting down hard at the base of his neck. Despite the deep wound, he tossed her off him and had time to deliver a few swift kicks to Peter's gut before Zara could make another attempt to stop him.

Despite her powerful martial art moves, the man was just too large and every kick and hit had little effect on him. Then she spotted the rusting farm tools in the corner and grabbed the pitchfork, but when she turned to save Peter from further blows, she was faced with two larger men who dwarfed her.

The taller of the two grabbed the pitchfork and easily snapped it in two. "I don't like to fight a woman," he said.

"Perfect," Zara said as she jumped up and kicked the man in the groin. Shocked, she just stared at him as he didn't even flinch.

"But I will if I have to," he added as he reached out and grabbed her by the throat.

Air barely got through to her lungs and the bright rays of the sun quickly dimmed until the ugly face of the man in front of her faded. Just when she thought she was going to pass out, she heard the distinct clink of a chain, then saw the expression on the man's face change as the chain wrapped around his neck. He immediately released her and tried to pull himself free of the death grasp.

"Leo," Zara said when she saw him standing behind the tall man, a long length of chain in his hand.

With a firm yank, he pulled the man back and off his feet.

"Leo, they're going to kill Peter."

Without stopping to consider his own safety, Leo turned to deliver the same punishment to the two men who were pummeling Peter. Bloodied and knocked out, Peter no longer offered any resistance at all.

In the distance, Zara heard the roar of more motor vehicles. "Hurry, Leo," she said as he slapped Peter back to wakefulness. "More cars are coming."

Peter came to and slapped Leo away. "What the bloody hell are you doing here?"

"Hey, you're welcome," Leo shot back.

"Stop bickering and let's get out of here," Zara said as she headed to the large open barn doors.

"My car's back here." Leo pointed to the back door.

But the black cars were already closing in.

"Go Zara," Peter said as he pushed her toward Leo. "I'll slow them down."

"No."

Peter looked at Leo. "Get her out of here."

"Peter," Zara argued. "No."

With a final glare at Leo, Peter turned and headed to the large barn doors.

"We have to stay," Zara said.

Leo didn't bother arguing with her, but just grabbed her wrist and dragged her out, but when a gunshot rang out, they both stopped to look back.

Peter stumbled, clutching his chest as blood oozed through his fingers.

278

Zara brought both hands over her grimacing mouth as tears sped to her eyes. "No," she muttered feebly as she watched Peter fall to his knees. She pushed Leo away and tried to run to Peter.

"Zara come back! It's too late, and Peter wanted you to get away safely," Leo said, tugging her toward his car.

"Peter!" she cried.

"Zara   Come on."

Tears streamed down her cheeks as she stared at Peter's body, waiting for Leo to guide her back to his car. She knew he was right; there was nothing they could do for Peter, yet the thought of leaving him there...

But Leo was suddenly silent and completely immobile. Zara turned to find him staring at his uncle, who had blocked them from Leo's car.

"You shouldn't have come out here, dear nephew."

Chapter 22

Leo

Leo stared at his uncle, the man who'd helped raise him, the man he'd always looked up to. Uncle Qingshan was the fun uncle, so cool and laid back compared to Leo's strict and rigid father. But as he thought back to those years so far away, he vaguely remembered a darker side to his father's younger brother. On more than one occasion Qingshan'd been on the wrong side of the law, but he'd always had an excuse. It was never his fault.

"What are you going to do, kid? Fight me?" He calmly reached for Leo's car keys.

"No matter what you've done, you're still my father's brother," Leo said with minimal reverence.

"Is that really the reason, or is it because you know I can whip your ass, even at fifty-six?"

Leo chuckled.

"You forget who taught you, Leo. I know every move you know, and then a few that you don't." Qingshan laughed, a sinister and mocking laugh that was devoid of any family ties. "You were only five years old when I started teaching you, and I have to admit it was sometimes really amusing. You were such a squirt, a little pint of a kid."

"I grew up big and strong, Uncle. You're making the mistake of underestimating your opponent, something you told me never to do."

Qingshan laughed again, this time with pure amusement. "Yes. Yes, I did say that, didn't I?"

"Give yourself up, Uncle. It's over."

"You know what they say, kid. It's not over until…"

Zara suddenly lunged at the older man. "…until the young lady whips butt." She landed both feet on the older man's chin and he fell back without any resistance. "You might not be able to fight him," she told Leo, "but I certainly can."

"Hurry," he said. "We've got to get out of here before…"

Something warm and hard clamped down at the back of his neck and spun him around.

"Hey, kid," the big burly man said. "Remember me?"

Leo immediately recognized him, as well as his companion who now held Zara in the same vice grip. They'd been students in his uncle's martial arts class, students who'd regularly tormented him.

"Who would have thought Uncle Qingshan was training his own future henchmen?" Leo said.

"He was a pretty good teacher, he even let us vent a little frustration on his pintsize nephew."

Leo tried to squirm free, but the hold on his neck was relentless. Closing his eyes, he concentrated. He knew they had to have a weak spot somewhere. His eyes flashed open and he looked to Zara, his eyes wide as he silently transmitted his message by letting his eyes trail down to the man's knees, and she instantly took the cue.

One after the other, they jumped up and landed their heels in their captors' knees. While the men cried out and fell to the ground, Leo grabbed her hand and ran. In the distance he saw a wooden fence, about six feet high, he estimated. They should be able to easily jump it.

"Hurry."

She bolted forward and he quickened the pace to keep up with her.

"I'm going to toss you over," he said as he intertwined his fingers, offering her a makeshift step.

Putting her foot in his hands, she climbed up and was atop the fence, ready to help Leo up, but he was quickly surrounded by the two henchmen who'd recovered all too quickly.

They concentrated on fighting Leo, and while he held his own, Zara jumped in. Flying off the fence, she landed on one of the henchmen, surprising him enough to knock him to the ground. For good measure, she kicked him a few solid times and turned around just in time to face a third man who promptly punched her in the face.

"I usually don't like punching a girl, but…"

Reeling, she staggered back while her head resonated from the blow. Her eyesight was momentarily tunneled, and Leo dutifully took up the fight, throwing each man down one after another.

She finally shook off the dizzy spell and jumped back in the melee. "You call that a punch," she hissed at her assailant just as she twisted around and kicked him with the back of her heel.

Two more men joined the fight and Zara let out a war cry as she focused her energies and got into an intense fight zone. She thought of Peter, and she was filled with rage. She kicked two men in the groin with a split kick, twisted in mid-air and elbowed the face of one, while landing on top of another on his shoulders, while her thighs crushed his head to the point of unconsciousness. She jumped off the man as he fell down, and ran to another, using her feet to run and kick the man's entire body as she used his weight against his own body. With one final kick, she knocked his chin back, forcing him to fall backward unconscious. One by one, the men, so much larger than she, fell to the ground able to do little more than groan.

Leo watched her with awe and amazement, impressed by her intensity and ferocity. He'd feared for her safety, but realized he needn't worry about her at all. He ducked in time to avoid the blow of another goon, while Zara simultaneously punched two men by sending her fists back on either side of her. She quickly turned around and kicked another man in the balls, sending him crumbling to the ground, tears streaking down his face.

Another man, screaming wildly, ran into the melee, but Zara silenced him with a solid blow to the head that nearly snapped his neck. "That's for Peter," she shouted as tears streamed down her cheeks. She repeatedly punched the downed man in the chest, shouting Peter's name over and over again.

With the last of them lying in pain on the ground, Leo came to Zara's side. "Those are some powerful legs you've got there."

Grinning, she winked and gave him an up and down glance. "So you better watch yourself, Leopold Lee."

"Yeah." He could just imagine her strong legs wrapped around him. He could imagine their bodies naked and sweating as they tangled together with unbridled passion. As he imagined the scene, a sharp, stinging blow hit the back of his head and he fell forward. On all fours, he tried to recuperate from the blow, but as he got to his knees, he was struck with a more painful blow; that of seeing Zara fall from a near fatal blow.

A well-dressed leg had directed an elegantly shoed foot right in Zara's chest, zapping the breath right out of her. Leo gasped when the attacker turned around.

UNASSUMED

Uncle Qingshan. The man he trusted the most in the world had just possibly killed the woman he loved beyond any conditions.

Seething, Leo got to his feet.

"You've pushed this too far, Uncle Qingshan." Certain his uncle wouldn't take up the fight with him, he walked up to him. He knelt beside Zara who tried to get up. "Stay where you are," he told her. "You need to catch your breath."

Glaring up at his uncle, he grimaced. "Haven't you hurt enough people, Unc... Argh. Qingshan?"

"Can't stomach the thought of calling me *uncle*, my dear nephew?" Qingshan's avuncular grin quickly turned sinister. "You've always been too emotional, Leo. It'll be the death of you."

"You've brought such shame to the Lee name."

"Naïve little man that you are. Maybe you should have taken your role as head of Lee Holdings more seriously, but no... you were off making movies and fucking starlets. You've always been a frivolous and silly child, and for all the money you've enjoyed and spent in your life, you have no idea how Lee Holdings manages to make so much money. Well let me tell you how... by constantly looking at the bottom line, and sometimes that bottom line just happens to slip under the strict line of the law.

"It is about making a profit wherever you can. It is about utilizing your resources. I have. I've maximized everything we've got including dealings with people who find use for our transportation methods. You have to learn that what I've done is best for the survival of this company. Those heirs...they were the frivolous ones, wasting the potential of their family companies. They have no business running their conglomerates just because their parents doted on them, and insisted they inherit the conglomerate without proper preparations. Years after those frivolous heirs take over, the run their family businesses to the ground. Years of hard work and sweat gone because of spoil brats like you, who inherit their parents' businesses without learning anything about them. They don't see it, but when they play these games of running conglomerates like it's a playground, when a factory closes, it is thousands of lives that are affected. Those people who work in the "transportation" department...they worked for Da Hwa once as our legitimate workers. They lost their jobs. They need to feed their families. Without any means, they turn to desperation and then to who will offer them a way to feed their families. That's where I come in. That's where I make a difference. You and all these young upstarts need wise advisers and leaders like me around to listen to. If not, then the rest of the conglomerates will fall. Think about that before you accuse anyone of anything."

"You can't justify what you've been doing," Zara 's voice rang out loud and clear as a bell. "How could you? Those severed fingers, Peter's death…how could you call that justice?"

"It's time to stop," Leo said. "Please Uncle or more lives will be lost." He looked at all the henchmen around. "Including these men, and their families. Do you all want to continue doing what you do instead of finding a safer more fulfilling life than hurting people?"

Looking dumbfounded, the men remained silent

Zara spoke again. "You killed an officer of the law. That is very serious offense," she looked at the men around her. "It could mean life in prison or even the death penalty. If you plead guilty now and give up and come peacefully with me to the station, it could mean less time in jail."

She pointed at Uncle Lee. "This man may be your Sifu, but surely you can think on your own. You don't have to listen to him. When you are in jail for life rotting away, what can he do for you? Don't think he'll save you. He'll only save himself. Think for yourself, and choose a better way of life. You can always change. There is still time."

The men grumbled and muttered among themselves and one of them finally turned to walk away. The remaining men looked briefly at Uncle Lee before walking away as well.

Uncle Lee stood facing Leo... alone.

"Come on Uncle," Leo said. "We're flesh and blood. We are all we have left in this world. Don't make me fight you."

UNASSUMED

"Your words are eloquent, Miss," Qingshan said to Zara, "but they have no effect on me. It's too late. I've made my choices and when you're in as deep as I am, there is no way out. I'm just the tip of the iceberg. This crime ring you've spent your entire life trying to find and defeat; it's so much larger than you can imagine. Your parents' death...it was planned, but I was not the one involved with that. Someone more powerful than I and more entrenched in your life and in everyone's life planned it. If you're really smart, you'll stop all investigations now."

Zara had to ask, "Why? What else is there? We got you, and you will confess everything to the police."

"No, I won't," Uncle Lee said, looking out beyond her and Leo. "You will continue looking. It is never-ending. Many of my beliefs come from men more powerful than I am. They run everything. Every single network. Every single existence you know. I am just a peg in their board. This is small time. There was France, there was Los Angeles...Oh, did I just say Los Angeles? Well, that hasn't happened yet. But..." A shot rang out of nowhere, and Uncle Lee fell to the ground, a bullet through his head.

"No!" Leo cried running to him. "Uncle, so sorry about everything. Please don't die. You're the only family I have left!"

Chapter 23

2 Weeks later

Zara

Zara settled into her new office at the Hong Kong police department and once again felt her heart grow heavy at the loss of Peter. Although his body wasn't recovered from the site he was killed, for some reason it had disappeared just as mysteriously as Leo's uncle being shot, they still held a memorial for him. Zara was heartbroken, realizing too late that she truly loved Peter. The weekend at Brockshire was magical, and she had fallen in love with Peter without a doubt then. His memorial service had been difficult, and while the entire Hong Kong force had come to show their respects, Zara had felt alone and lost.

That had been two weeks ago, and even with her new promotion, she had difficulty forcing a smile to all who congratulated her.

A rap at the door drew her attention. "Leo," she said with the same forced smile she offered everyone. "What brings you here?"

She hadn't seen him since the funeral.

He shrugged. "Just getting back to normal life."

"Despite the loss of your uncle, you must be relieved it's all over. Not to mention not having me following you around everywhere."

With everything that had happened, she'd almost forgotten what it'd been like being around him. Seeing him, she suddenly realized just how much she'd missed him.

"I don't know," he said. "I was getting used to having you around all the time." He looked around the new office that still had several unpacked boxes. "How 'bout some coffee?"

"Oh," she said with a relieved sigh. "I could really go for a good cup of coffee. My promotion hasn't improved the quality of coffee here."

They strolled in comfortable silence to the nearby coffee shop and, once there, Zara sat at a corner table while Leo headed to the counter to buy two mega cups of coffee.

"Perfect," she said when he handed her the oversized cup.

"How have you been doing?"

"There hasn't been a night that I haven't woken up with a vision of Peter falling back dead. I can't forget it. Peter. It's one thing to lose someone you love, but to actually see it... it's such a nightmare. Well, you would know, right?"

Leo nodded his understanding.

"This new promotion has kept me busy though," she went on. "As you could see from the state of my office, I haven't even had time to empty my boxes yet. I'm busy, busy, busy as the head of this new unit, and I like it that way. The busier I am, the less time I have to think about other things."

Reaching for her hand, Leo said, "He spoke often about you."

"Peter?"

Leo nodded. "He wanted me to stay away from you. He really loved you. Said he envisioned his life with you."

"He was a very good man, and I just didn't appreciate him enough. In the end, though, I realized too late how much I cared for him."

"I know I'm not Peter... Tell you the truth, I wasn't really a fan, but..."

"Jealous?" Zara said with the first sincere smile on her lips since Peter's death.

"Maybe a tad." Leo gave her hand a squeeze. "Look, I know I could never replace him, I mean, he was a decent guy. I mean, to stand up for his father even in light of the illegal activities he was involved in... well, I know it must have been difficult."

They stared into their coffee cups for a silent moment.

"And of course, he saved our lives," Leo said quietly. "I'll never forget that."

"Me neither."

"And I'll always be grateful for everything you've done for me. I know it was just all part of your job, but..."

"I've enjoyed working with you, Leo."

"Good," he said with a warm smile. He emptied his cup of coffee and gently set the large cup down. "I'd like to see you."

Zara didn't know what to say.

"Could we have dinner tonight?"

"Yes, but I must warn you, I'm still feeling fragile."

"I can take it."

"Fine then."

"Come to my place, eight o'clock. I've been working on a new dish and I can't wait to share it with someone." He leaned in to kiss her cheek. "You'll see, it's absolutely to die for."

His lips were soft, and she welcomed his touch.

They left the coffee shop and walked slowly down the street. She'd draped her hand through the crook of his arm, a motion that seemed so natural, yet platonic.

She liked the feel of him, his strength, his warmth.

"It isn't over," he softly said into her ear.

Staring straight ahead, she maintained a cool and unmoved expression, but her blood ran cold. His tone wasn't loving or teasing; it was deathly cold.

"Smile and look amused by my loving attention, but be aware; they're watching us. Uncle Qingshan was right. He was just a pawn. I'm just a pawn. I've been going through his stuff and I have so much to show you. Everything you know to be safe and comfortable is about to change."

Epilogue

Lord Brock – At Brockshire

"You can bring him out of the room now," Lord Brock called out. "It's safe."

Two men dressed in black helped a man dressed in a plush velvet navy blue robe walk out of a room hidden behind the library bookcase.

Lord Brock removed his tie and his suit jacket, settling down into his favorite leather sofa. An antique piece that had been in the family for hundreds of years.

"It's a little early to make an appearance anywhere, but for now, you can't show your face anywhere. If you do, you'd be dead for sure."

The man in the robe stared straight ahead, his eyes unflinching, unemotional.

"Good thing my men got to you before they did, retrieving you from the scene before they could make sure you would never talk."

Lord Brock poured himself some whiskey and took a stiff drink. "And once again, I was able to find a way out of any situation. Two weeks in jail for accepting bribes, then poof, all the proof disappears, and I'm a free man again. I told you, these men who I work with are powerful. They are in the highest echelon of all walks. If they knew I had saved you and was harboring you, nurturing you back to life; they would go after me, too. But as long as I'm still valuable to them. As long as I could still carry out my function, I live."

"I feel dead," an emotionless voice said. "I'd rather be dead if I can't have my life back and have to remain hiding away from the world who think I'm dead."

"What do you intend to do? Show yourself?" Lord Brock said. "They held a funeral for you already, and she's already moved on. Your little ex-fiance. Quite a test of love you put her through, with your death and all. She proved to be quite faithful and quite in love with you in the end. A true match for you, worthy of your love, son," Lord Brock said.

"It wasn't a test, Dad," Peter said. "She truly thought I'd died. I thought I'd died, but thanks to you,

I was grabbed by your men right when Quinshan was shot. Handy, Dad, handy. That's how you deal with "proof"? I didn't think you were capable, but now I know you are. Zara was right. She has an amazing instinct. Always has. I can't wait to see her again."

"You can't let her know you're alive."

"Then it isn't worth being alive, isn't it?" Peter said. "What if I suddenly make a resurrection from the dead?"

"You're an idiot, Peter. It would mean the death of you, me, and her."

"Her?" Peter asked. "Why?"

"Don't you get it, dense boy? They could've killed her in the factory that time she was kidnapped. They could have killed Leopold Lee anytime, especially since his uncle had access to him all the time. The reason why Leopold Lee and Zara are alive still is because of you, Peter. Because you're my son, and I want you to succeed. You cared for Zara, so she lives. And Leopold Lee is your case. Your responsibility to keep alive, so he lives."

"Why Dad?" Peter asked.

"Because," Lord Brock said, "A father will do everything for his son, including being sworn to secrecy into a society so ancient yet so powerful, it would ensure the legacy of their sons for generations to come. You're expected to take over my spot when I die, Peter. To carry out my role until your death, and then it passes on to your son and then to his.

"What is this society you speak of?" Peter asked. "What if I refuse to be part of it?"

"I can't tell you until it's time, and if you refuse to be part of it, you will find that you have no choice. Every road you take, every path you try will lead you right back to them."

"I can't be with Zara?" Peter asked.

"No, she's a Zee, an oppose to the society back in the time of the Qi Dynasty. It's not meant to be, and if you push it, you will find, you and her are destined to become enemies."

"

This is the end of UNASSUMED

*****

A new series based on Zara and Leo called UNASSUMED GIRL is set to release in December 2015 and will continue with Peter and a new cast of characters.

To be notified as soon as the next parts are released, please join the Kailin Gow Mailing List at http://www.kailingowbooks.com. Also, please feel free to like my Facebook page for more updates.

If you enjoyed this novel, please leave a review, and recommend it to a friend.

*****

Let her know by leaving stars and letting her know what you like about

UNASSUMED

*****

Other Books like HEAT

The Protege

For 18 and Up

A quick read, all three books in The Protégé Trilogy is available here:

http://www.amazon.com/Protege-Kailin-Gow-ebook/dp/B00C0TIQ0K

The Blue Room Series

Available Here:

http://www.amazon.com/Blue-Room-Vol-1-
ebook/dp/B00K7M775M/

When Danny Blue of the Never Knights inherited his playboy billionaire father's businesses and legacy, he didn't realized his father's pet project was the Blue Room, the most elite and secret club in the highest circle. He was happy to let his half-brother Terrence Blue run the club, but with Terrence's womanizing ways and carefree attitude when it came to everything, he wasn't sure if that was a good idea.

Terrence Blue wasn't sure that was a good idea as well because it would cramp his style as a former patron of the club, but when he spotted virginal Staci Atussi starting at The Blue Room, he had a change of heart. Not only was Staci Atussi a knockout without knowing it, but she was the challenge he had been craving.

For Staci Atussi, working at The Blue Room was her solution to a desperate situation, but as she became integrated into the world of The Blue Room and the mysteries surrounding its patrons and the sexy Blues, she wondered if she had traded in her desperation for something far more sinister.

The Blue Room is a New Adult Contemporary Suspense Series intended for readers age 18 and up.

DON'T MISS IT!

To ensure you don't miss Kailin Gow's next book, join the site at Sparklesoup.com where you can get more information about books similar to UNASSUMED and more!

WANT MORE? LET US KNOW. KAILIN GOW'S BOOKS ARE FAN DRIVEN. JOIN THE DISCUSSION AT:

**FACEBOOK
(http://www.facebook.com/OfficialKailinGow)**